SHADOWED

ALSO BY CARL DEUKER

SHADOWED

CARL DEUKER

CLARION BOOKS
An Imprint of HarperCollins*Publishers*

For Imogen

The author would like to thank Mary Wilcox
and Amy Cloud, the editors of this book, for
their guidance and encouragements

Clarion Books is an imprint of HarperCollins Publishers.

Shadowed

www.epicreads.com
Library of Congress Control Number: 2023948583
ISBN 978-0-06-337634-2
Typography by Julia Tyler
24 25 26 27 28 LBC 5 4 3 2 1
FIRST EDITION

BEFORE

1

BEFORE I GET TO BASKETBALL and Creepy Crawley and all that, you need to understand that soccer has always been a religion in my house. In my baby pictures, I'm wearing a Seattle Sounders jersey. My parents stuck me on my first team when I was five. Before matches, my mom always said, "Nate, come back with your shield—or on it." I didn't get it until my sister, Amelia, told me that Caesar said that to his soldiers before battle. "It means, 'Win or die,'" she explained. Mom was smiling, but it wasn't entirely a joke.

My parents hoped that both Amelia and I would score soccer scholarships. A big-time college was their dream, but Southwest Louisiana State, if there is such a school, would work, too. We're not poor, but nobody gets rich owning submarine sandwich shops, which is what my parents do.

Amelia—she's two years older than me—is one of *those* sisters. Great athlete. A+ student. Swedish Hospital Volunteer of the Year. Blah, blah, blah. At Salmon Bay K–8, teachers' and coaches' eyes lit up when they learned I was Amelia's brother. Once they got to know me, the light dimmed. I'm not a bad student or a bad athlete—I'm just not Amelia.

2

I SHOULD HAVE KNOWN THAT basketball is my game. At Salmon Bay, the best athletes in my class were Colin Vatonen and Bo Dietz. I've never liked Colin, and I only sort of get along with Bo. No reason, really; that's just the way it is.

Colin is tall, with surfer-boy hair and long arms. His father, who played on Finland's Olympic national team, was drafted in the second round by the Oklahoma City Thunder. The Thunder cut him, but he played eleven years in Europe before moving to Seattle.

When you're the best athlete in a school that goes from kindergarten through eighth grade, you call the shots. Colin wanted to play basketball, so every day we played basketball. Since Colin wanted Bo Dietz on his team, that happened, too.

I'm not saying that Bo—dark-haired, stocky—isn't a good athlete, but he wasn't better than me at hoops. He lives next door to Colin up in Sunset Hill, the fancy part of Ballard, and he has always been totally okay with being the guy who sets the screens and makes the passes that set Colin up to score a zillion points and be the star.

In grade school, I liked the challenge of taking Colin on. I never had any basketball coaching, but I could shoot and dribble, which made me captain of the other team. Most games we got crushed, but sometimes I'd catch fire, knock down a bunch of shots, and we'd win. Colin hated losing to me as much as I loved beating him.

3

THE STUFF WITH LUCAS CAWLEY started when Mr. Krebs, the old guy across the street who let me feed his chickens, had a stroke. The night of Amelia's eighth-grade graduation, we returned home to see him being loaded into an ambulance on a stretcher. Two days later his daughter came by to pick up the chickens and to tell my parents that her father was at a rehabilitation center. "He'll be back in a few months," my mom told her. "Your dad is tough." A few months went by and then a few more, and then it was a year.

A weird thing about houses is that they fall apart if no one lives in them. Moss grew on Mr. Krebs's roof; the paint peeled; weeds took over the lawn and flower beds. One night in early June, burglars pried open the door to his shed and stole his tools.

Mr. Krebs's daughter had the shed door fixed. Before she left, she put a For Rent sign in front of the house. "Who would live in that dump?" Amelia asked my mom.

"It'll be cheap," Mom answered, "so that'll help. It can't rent fast enough, as far as I'm concerned."

Mom got her wish. The Cawleys moved in on the last day of school.

4

A NEW KID MOVES IN across the street, you notice. I spotted Lucas, saw he was about my age, and went over. After the first time, I did it pretty much every afternoon that summer, until the day came when I didn't.

You've probably already figured out that my family is boringly normal. There is nothing normal about the Cawleys. First off, Lucas calls his father *Bill* and told me to call him *Bill*, too. Who does that?

Bill is a beat-up version of Lucas. They both have long, bony faces and gray-green eyes. Bill also has a long, ratty beard and even longer ratty hair. But, while Lucas's eyes are on high alert, his father's eyes always seem to be looking at something nobody else can see.

Bill's job—if you can call it a job—was making planter boxes and trellises for Sky Nursery. All day every day he was pounding and hammering and sawing. Lucas and I would help him by carrying the lumber in or holding boards steady or getting screws or nails. Sometimes, in the middle of doing something, Bill would just stop and stare into space. Then we'd wait.

While the hammering was going on, Lucas's twin sister, Megan—dark hair, dark eyes, and pale skin—sat up on the top of a ladder and watched. Sometimes, for no reason that I could see, she'd start clapping her hands and laughing. Whenever she did that, Lucas would go over and high-five her. I tried to high-five her once, but she turned away and covered her face. "Leave her alone," Lucas said, so I did.

Richard, Lucas's older brother, spent most days riding his fire-engine red Kawasaki Ninja, with Sara, his girlfriend, holding on tight. Some days, though, he'd be in the corner of the shed working on his motorcycle, listening to Drake or Jay-Z, sweat running down his tattooed arms. Sara would sit on a stool and smoke. She was everything my parents didn't want Amelia to be—red-green hair, heavy makeup, and skimpy tops that she only half buttoned. Whenever she caught me staring at her, she'd smile and blow smoke my way.

Right after they moved in, Bill lopped off some drooping branches and nailed a basketball hoop into the corkscrew willow that was their street tree. Around three o'clock Bill would stop pounding nails and disappear into the house, leaving Lucas and me to shoot hoops in the street. The hoop was too high and a little crooked, and the trunk of a tree doesn't make much of a backboard, but it didn't matter.

We'd go one-on-one. I was the better shooter, but he was a bloodhound going after loose balls and rebounds, so the games were even. Megan was with us, and Lucas made sure she got her turn. She'd shoot once in a while, but mainly she'd bounce the ball and watch as it soared up and over her head. Sometimes she'd jump with the ball, as if it were pulling her up, up, up.

I don't know much about Lucas's mother. From things he said, I figured out that she worked the night shift at University of Washington Hospital and slept during the day. I get that she wouldn't be up much, but never coming outside at all? Nobody in the house cooked, because every night they got Domino's or McDonald's or something like that delivered. Lucas would take the food from the delivery driver, Megan would follow him into the house, and that ended our one-on-one game.

5

SO, HERE'S THE AUGUST AFTERNOON when everything changes. Lucas's mother is sleeping; Richard and Sara are flying around on his motorcycle. Bill is sawing away, with Lucas and me helping and Megan watching from her perch. Out of nowhere, the sky suddenly goes dark, the temperature drops, and I hear thunder. Minute by minute the wind grows stronger and louder until it's a roar. Lucas looks at Megan. "You want to feel the wind?" he asks.

She nods and comes down off the ladder. He takes her hand, pushes open the shed door, and leads her outside. I trail behind.

By now the trees are swaying, and stray bits of paper are tumbling down the street. Seagulls are dipping their wings, gliding with the current, almost as if they're playing. Megan opens her arms and faces the wind, her eyes electric. Every few seconds she jumps up and down, claps her hands, and then opens her arms to embrace the wind.

My heart rate jumped when I'd first heard the thunder, but

then it went back to normal. That doesn't happen for Megan. For her, every second is as thrilling as the first.

"What exactly is wrong with her, anyway?" I whisper to Lucas.

He turns on me. "There's nothing wrong with her."

"Okay," I answer. "If you say so."

"What's that supposed to mean?" he says, his eyes flashing.

I smile. "Come on, Lucas. Anybody can see she's not—"

I do see his fist coming, so I manage to duck. Still, the punch catches me on the side of my neck and sends me sprawling. My ears are ringing, and I'm trying to catch my breath when he kicks me in the ribs . . . once, twice, three times. That's when Megan starts wailing. Lucas stops, looks at me as I lie there in the dirt, and then grabs her by the hand and leads her back into the shed.

I lie there for a while before I get up and stumble home. I hope to sneak up to my room, but Amelia, who'd been watching a soccer game on TV with her friend Alice, knows something is wrong as soon as I step inside.

"What happened to you?" she asks, scrunching up her face and rising to her feet. "Your neck is all red. And why are you bent over like that?" She pauses. "Nate, have you been crying?"

"I'm okay," I say, but she makes me sit on the sofa.

"You're not okay. You can't even stand straight. I'm calling Mom."

6

IT'S MY DAD WHO COMES home. As we drive to Tallman Medical, he makes me describe what had gone down. The only thing I leave out is the part where I smiled.

Dr. Charles sends me for X-rays, and it turns out my ribs are bruised, not broken. "Go easy for a while," he says. "A heating pad or a hot-water bottle will help, but time is the real cure."

Back home, Mom meets us at the front door. Dad had called and filled her in while I was getting X-rays. "I'm going over there to talk to Lucas's parents right now," Dad says to her.

"Don't!" I say, but he turns and heads out.

When he comes back, he huddles with Mom in the kitchen, their voices low. After they finish, they call a family meeting. We're supposed to have one every week, but I don't think we've had one for a year.

This isn't a meeting either; they just lay down rules. "You want to have Lucas over here, that's okay," Dad says, "but you don't go over there anymore. Understood?"

"I don't want to do anything with him ever," I say. "Here or there."

Dad turns to Amelia. "And as for you."

"Me? What do I have to do with this?" Amelia says.

"Nothing. And we want it to stay that way. So steer clear of Lucas's brother."

Her eyes go wide. "His brother? Why would I have anything to do with him? I don't even know his name."

Mom jumps in. "His name is Richard. And all we're saying is that if he offers you a ride on his motorcycle or asks you to go for a walk, or anything like that, it's 'No.' Understood?"

"I wouldn't go out with him," Amelia snaps. "He's a loser."

"Then there's no problem," Mom says, but Amelia's eyes stay angry.

7

A COUPLE DAYS GO BY, and then Amelia, clutching her laptop, taps on my door and slips inside my room. She puts her laptop on my desk and opens it up. "I googled the Cawleys," she says.

"What?"

"I googled them."

"Why?"

"Because Mom and Dad are acting so weird. I thought maybe they're criminals or something."

"Are they?"

"The opposite. At least for Mr. Cawley." She pauses. "He's an Afghanistan war hero."

"Bill? A war hero?"

"You call him Bill?"

I shrug. "That's what Lucas told me to call him, so, yeah, that's what I call him. But there's no way he's a war hero. It must be some other Bill Cawley."

"Look," she says, pointing to a photo on her computer screen.

"That's him, right? Okay, no long hair and no beard, but those eyes are unmistakable. And that's President Obama giving him the Medal of Honor. They only give that to soldiers who save other soldiers. The article says he has a Purple Heart, too, which means he was wounded."

I shake my head. "It's hard to believe. He seems so out of it."

Amelia scowls. "Come on, Nate, get a clue. He's got PTSD from the war. And the way he is probably explains why the mother drinks."

That startles me. "How do you know she drinks?"

Amelia closes her laptop and lowers her voice. "This is going to sound like I was snooping, but I wasn't. It just happened."

"What just happened?"

"Alice and I were coming back from Larsen's—this was maybe a month ago."

"Yeah. So?"

"So, we'd finished our lattes, and the Cawleys' recycling bin was out on the street, which is totally normal for them. I opened it so we could toss in our cups, and there had to be ten empty vodka bottles in there. Since then, whenever we pass by, we peek, and it's always full of vodka bottles." She pauses, and the tone of her voice changes. "I feel sorry for Lucas. Maybe after a while, you could have him over."

I gape at her. "Not happening," I say.

She shrugs. "Well, I just thought if you knew the whole story, it might change things."

"It doesn't. As far as I'm concerned, the guy does not exist."

8

WHEN SCHOOL STARTED, MY PARENTS did what parents are supposed to do. They got me new clothes, a new backpack, new notebooks and pens and paper. Lucas showed up at Salmon Bay K–8 wearing beat-up jeans, a beat-up shirt, beat-up shoes. It turned out he's a year younger than me, so I had no classes with him, but I did see him on the playground and in the cafeteria. Half the time it didn't seem like he had any lunch at all, which is probably why he took on the look of a coyote—skinny but strong, with alert eyes.

Megan was also at Salmon Bay, but she spent her day in C Wing, which is where the special-needs kids had their classes. The few times I saw her on her own in the hallways, her eyes were fixed on the ground and her shoulders were slumped.

Here's how the Creepy Crawley thing started. Instead of hanging out with the kids in his class, during any free time Lucas would go to the C Wing to be with Megan. They'd bounce a ball together; he'd push her on the swings; they'd climb around on the ropes and the jungle gym.

One day in early October, the two of them did a caterpillar crawl together—arms stretched forward, then knees drawn up, butts in the air, then arms stretched forward, then knees drawn up, butts in the air—around the edge of the C Wing play area. We could see them from the basketball court. "That's that Cawley kid, isn't it?" Colin said. "And his weird sister. What are they doing?"

Nobody answered, and we went back to our game, but Lucas and Megan started up again the next day. "Hey, Creepy Crawley, looking good!" Colin called out, getting a big laugh from everyone.

Lucas was close, so he had to have heard the name and the laughter. If I'd been him, I'd have been on my feet in a tenth of a second, and I'd never do the caterpillar crawl thing again. Not Lucas, though. He kept right on doing what he was doing, not just that day, but whenever Megan asked, which is why the *Creepy Crawley* tag stuck.

I never called Lucas that—my parents drilled into me that you don't ridicule people—but I never told Colin or anybody else to stop. Okay, taking all that ridicule for his sister took guts. Still, the guy sucker punched me and then kicked me when I was lying on the ground. Why should I stand up for him?

9

I'LL DO THE REST OF that year in fast-forward. I do okay in my classes, Bs, with an A in PE. I play hoops against Colin and Bo during any free time. I make the boys' soccer team—barely—and play a few minutes in a few games. I make a summer semi-select soccer team—barely—and play a few minutes in a few games. Amelia gets all As, is a starter on Shilshole High's soccer team, a starter on her select soccer team. She's thinking college scholarship, and my parents are thinking the same thing. Lucas Cawley shoots around in front of his house every afternoon after school, and sometimes again under the street-lights at night. I feel the pull of the ball and the hoop and those one-on-one games we had, but I don't talk to him, and he never says a word to me.

The only other thing that happens is Hanna Hadera. Her family moved to Seattle from Ethiopia when she was in kin-dergarten. She's skinny, and she's got zits on her forehead, and she's also smart and funny and athletic, and when I'm not thinking about starting high school, I'm thinking about her. Every August, a bunch of Salmon Bay kids all take the same swimming class at Blue Ridge Pool. I talk to Hanna a little, but not as much as I want. Most of the time she's with Colin and Bo.

10

ON MY FIRST DAY AT Shilshole High, Ms. Clyburn, the principal, meets with all the freshmen to tell us how welcome we are. "I know some of you might be a little nervous, but let me assure you, this is a safe place. You belong here."

It sounds good, but half the senior guys in the hallways look like men, and half of that half look like convicts. *All* the senior girls look like women, making me feel like a third grader. For weeks, I don't feel like I belong at all.

By October, though, things are okay. The schoolwork is harder than it had been at Salmon Bay, but not massively more difficult, and the kids in my classes are my age, so there's nothing scary about them.

Girls' soccer is a fall sport, so from the first week of school Amelia's name comes through the intercom at the beginning of each day. She'd been a starter as a sophomore, but she took off as a junior, scoring at least one goal in each of the first ten games and leading the team to the Metro League playoffs, where they lost in the semifinals.

I'd be lying if I said I'm not jealous, but being Amelia Dravus's little brother is better than being nobody. Whenever she sees me in the hallway, she comes over and talks to me. Lots of kids at the school have older brothers and sisters who never give them a nod.

The other name I heard constantly over the intercom in late fall and winter is as grating as the sound of a dentist's drill—Colin Vatonen, the leading scorer for the freshman basketball team in game after winning game.

11

MY FATHER'S PARENTS MOVED TO Portugal when they retired. Nobody ever says it, but I don't think they have much money, and Portugal is cheaper than the USA. I talk to them sometimes on FaceTime, and they seem nice enough, but they never visit. My dad says that some year we'll go to Portugal, but it hasn't happened yet.

The grandparents who do come every Christmas are my mother's parents. They live in Missoula, where Grandfather Frick was a judge and Grandmother Frick was on the school board for something like thirty years. They belong to a country club and take cruises all the time. Grandmother Frick doesn't say much, but Grandfather Frick always makes jokes about the submarine shops—"I hope they don't go under" is his favorite—that rub my parents the wrong way.

One thing about having rich grandparents—they give good gifts. For Christmas, I get the new PlayStation console and a bunch of FIFA video games. My parents give me a new pair of soccer shoes, a book about Lionel Messi, and some goalie gloves. I'd played goalie a few times, and they know I hated it—boring, boring, boring.

My dad catches the puzzled look on my face. "At least think about it, Nate," he says. "Shilshole High is much bigger than Salmon Bay, which means more guys going out. You've got good hands—goalie might be your best shot at making the team."

I nod—message delivered. My parents think I suck on the field.

12

AS TRYOUTS APPROACH, AMELIA'S SUCCESS on the girls' team gives me hope. If she's gone from great to superstar, I could go from okay to good.

About three dozen guys turn out for the freshman team. I tell Coach Whaley, a tall guy with red hair pulled back in a man bun, that I want to play fullback. When he calls out for goalies, I don't raise my hand.

I give it my all that first day, but walking home, I know I didn't take any miraculous leap forward. Ten guys are solid, about the same number are hopeless, and the other sixteen are like me—mediocre players who might make the team but might not. Flip of the coin.

I don't like soccer, but I do like sitting in the section of the cafeteria with the other athletes, especially since Hanna—who is a volleyball and track star—is there. If I get cut, I won't fit. And if I don't fit with the athletes, where do I fit?

x x x

"I can play goalie," I tell Coach Whaley the next day.

His eyebrows go up. "Have you played before?"

"Some. At Salmon Bay K–8 and on rec teams." I pause. "I've got good hands."

"Glad to hear it," he says with a smile. "Don't want a goalie who can't catch." He points to the north end of the field. "I'll check in now and again, but mainly you'll be working with Ms. Freund. She played goalie at Bellevue College, so she knows her stuff."

It takes about one minute for me to know I made a smart decision. My competition drops from sixteen guys to two— Max Grillo and Brant Moore. Grillo is long-armed, quick, and experienced; I'm not beating him out. Moore, though, seems as if he's never played soccer. Ms. Freund keeps reminding him not to stand behind the goal line, and he flat-out whiffs a couple of free kicks. "My dad made me try out," he admits to me. "I hope I get cut."

He gets his wish.

Two days later I come home with the news that I've made the team, bringing smiles to the faces of my parents and earning me a cheeseburger, fries, and milkshake at the Red Mill on Greenwood.

That turns out to be the highlight of my season.

The only position on a team more boring than goalie is second-string goalie. Coach Whaley promises I'll get time whenever a game is out of reach—either we're way behind or way ahead. We don't score much, but Grillo is solid, so our opponents never score much either. 2–1. 2–0. 3–2. 1–0.

A whole season of close games.

A whole season of sitting on the bench.

I keep eating lunch in the athletes' section of the cafeteria even though I know I'm a fraud. I have the uniform, but Lucas Cawley—shooting for hours at the hoop Bill nailed to the corkscrew willow—is more of an athlete than me.

13

THAT SUMMER, MOM AND DAD drag me along on what they pretend is a vacation but what is really a scholarship search for Amelia. "We've got to get your name out there," Mom says to her. "And after the year you've had, coaches will be interested."

The trip is a total yawner for me, but Amelia meets coaches and sees schools from Seattle to San Diego. When the head coaches aren't around, my parents make sure that someone in the athletic department gets a DVD of Amelia's highlights. "She came into her own this past year," they take turns saying, "and next year she'll skyrocket."

When we return home, two schools call back—Portland and Cal Berkeley. Neither promise anything, but both want regular updates. "Do you know how good a school Cal is?" Amelia asks me in an excited whisper. "I can't believe they're interested in me."

She's always been a hard worker, but after those phone calls she's nonstop. When she isn't practicing or playing a game with her select team, she's at the community center working out with Mom or Dad. Most of the time, I'm guilted into going along. "You can practice your goalkeeping while you help your sister. What else do you have to do?"

Then a weird thing happens—the more Amelia practices, the worse she does. At Shilshole High, she was leading scorer, her shots routinely finding the back of the net. On her summer team, her shots are wide left, wide right, high, or right at the goalie. "You're guiding everything," my mom says. "You've got to let it go, free and easy."

Amelia hits rock bottom at a Saturday tournament in North Bend the first week of August. Her team plays two games, and she has six great shots on goal and misses all six. I'm not there, but I hear about it when she returns home. "The Cal coach wants updates," she says to me. "If I had scored even once . . ." She pauses. "Honest to God, Nate, I don't think I'll ever score another goal in my life."

14

SUNDAY, MOM IS ALL SMILES. "No feeling sorry for yourself," she says to Amelia, clapping her hands together while she's finishing her breakfast. "You're going to put the ball in the net again. It's just a matter of time."

In the afternoon she makes me go with her and Amelia to the community center to practice. She sticks me in goal while she teaches Amelia a new move. "Be ready," she says to me.

It's a spin move, and Amelia tries and fails a dozen times. And I mean total fails—her shots are nowhere near the goal. Her face grows tight with frustration, and so does Mom's. For me, watching her miss and miss is just boring, which is why I stop paying attention. Then—and I think I saw it about a millisecond before contact—the soccer ball smashes me square in the face, and I go down.

When I come to, I'm on my side, blood pouring from my nose. I try to sit up, but I go right back down, my brain still bouncing around inside my skull.

You hear about concussions, but you don't really know what they are until you have one. I know we went to the emergency room, and I think I heard some talk of staying overnight, which didn't happen.

Back home, I remember eating soup, but not what kind, and I remember wanting to sleep and having either Mom or Dad wake me up every hour or so.

I feel okay in the morning until the headache sneaks up on me like a rogue wave. Everything is calm, and then—from nowhere—it overwhelms me.

My mom takes me to see Dr. Charles at the Tallman clinic. "A concussion is a brain injury," he says. "You wouldn't mess around with a sprained ankle—you'd let it heal. It's even more important with your brain. Don't push it."

"He's got swim class at Blue Ridge in a couple of weeks," my mom says. "Do you think he'll be—"

"Maybe," Dr. Charles says, "but these things are tough to predict."

I don't like hearing *maybe*. Colin and Bo will be at Blue Ridge, but so will Hanna. I didn't talk with her much last summer, but I'm determined to change that, maybe even ask her to hang out after swimming. Go to Green Lake or down to Carkeek Park or Golden Gardens—something like that.

I know about football players and the concussion protocol they go through. Some guys play the next week; other guys miss the season. Mine has to be the no-big-deal concussion. It just has to be.

15

EVERYBODY THINKS SEATTLE'S WEATHER SUCKS, and the winters do, but August is warm, not too hot, and it doesn't get dark until after eight. I go outside every morning, walk a little, and then try jogging. After ten minutes or so, the headache comes, driving me back into my room. I can't play video games, because the flashing lights are like jets of fire burning through my eyeballs. Listening to my tunes is the same, but there the fire scorches my eardrums.

Most days, my parents are either at work or watching Amelia play soccer, leaving me alone. In the afternoon, after Bill stops his sawing and pounding, I hear the *thump-thump-thump* of a basketball.

Lucas and Megan.

I go to the window and watch. He drives to the hoop, takes pull-up jump shots, practices free throws, and then shares the ball with Megan. She bounces the ball and jumps up with it, smiling. Sometimes, though, the ball hits her foot or the curb and goes bounding off. She clenches her fists by her cheeks in frustration, but Lucas quickly runs it down, brings it back to her, and lets her have another go at it.

The day before Blue Ridge swimming starts, I walk over to Loyal Heights Community Center. No headache. I get a basketball from the guy behind the counter, take a few shots in the gym, and then drive the length of the court for a lay-in. After the ball goes through the net, I lean over to pick it up. When I straighten, my head feels like it's about to explode, and I almost throw up.

Blue Ridge isn't happening.

16

MY HEADACHES ARE STILL BAD when I start my sophomore year. The first day, as I'm carefully pulling my backpack over my shoulder, I glance out the window. Lucas and Megan are side by side, waiting. Waiting for what? I wonder. Then I get it. Echohawk High, not Shilshole, has the special ed program for the north end of Seattle. Megan would be going there.

A small yellow school bus pulls up. Megan hangs on to Lucas's arm like a kindergarten kid hanging on to her mom. Lucas gets on the bus with her and talks with the bus driver. As soon as he gets off, he rushes to Megan's window and presses his hands against the glass. She puts her hands on the glass, mirroring his. When the bus drives off, he waves after it. It isn't until it disappears around the corner that he heads to Shilshole for his first day of high school.

I wait a few minutes before I leave. The anger I felt over the beating he gave me is gone, but there is no way I'm going to be seen walking to Shilshole High with Creepy Crawley.

17

ALL SEPTEMBER, THE HEADACHES COULD hit from out of nowhere like a lightning bolt from the sky, so I stay clear of the noise that fills the cafeteria and the main hallway. Sometimes I can't follow the lessons, especially in math and biology, but I don't know whether that's because of the concussion or because the subject matter is hard. PE has always been my favorite class, but Dr. Charles limits me to light stretches and walking, which I do alone out on the track.

What sucks most is not knowing how long all this will last. Every day when I get home from school, I pull down the blinds, close my door, and lie on my bed in the dark. I can hear Lucas outside on the street as he dribbles and shoots at that miserable hoop nailed to the tree.

Girls' soccer season starts, and Amelia scores a goal in the first minute of the first game, which opens the floodgates. I could go to her games and sit apart from the screaming parents, but it would be torture to watch her running around when I can't even lean over.

I hear all about her games, though. She scores thirteen goals in her first ten games, and Shilshole High wins them all. My parents print up the *Seattle Times* articles and mail them off to every school we visited over the summer.

In the second half of the season, Amelia stays hot, but the team's number one goalkeeper suffers one of those high-ankle sprains that take months to heal. Her replacement is Paige Truly, a sophomore. "She's good in practice," Amelia worries, "but games are different."

She's right to be anxious; Shilshole finishes with four straight losses and misses the Metro playoffs.

After Amelia's final game, we sit around the kitchen table putting together one last packet that contains news articles, a DVD of her senior-year highlights, a copy of her report card, and a letter from her head coach. When all the envelopes are ready, I go to the post office with my dad.

He notices that I'm glum. "I know it seems like it's nonstop Amelia, but you'll be good to play soccer in the spring, and we'll be there for you. You'll see."

I want to tell him that I'm done with soccer, but I know that would make him mad, then I'd get mad, we'd argue, and I'd end up with a roaring headache, so I take the easy way out. "I'm not jealous," I tell him. "I'm just sick of being sick."

18

THOSE ARE NERVOUS DAYS AT home. After sending out her DVD, Amelia gets slews of emails from coaches, who all say basically the same thing: "We liked what we saw on your DVD. You're just the kind of student-athlete that would fit our program." Every email sounds incredibly positive, but none include a scholarship offer.

Then, early in December, Amelia pounds on my door and then throws it open. "Come downstairs with me!" she almost shouts. "I've got news."

Once she has us assembled in the front room, she looks at my mom and dad and then at me. "I got a phone call from Coach Nguyen at Cal." She pauses for effect. I can see my parents' eyes light up. "He offered me a scholarship. Well, half a scholarship. He wants me to talk to you tonight, sleep on it, and then call him back with an answer tomorrow. I can say yes, can't I?"

I look to my parents. I think they'd be crazy happy, but the earlier excitement in their eyes changes to a look of pain. Finally, my mom shakes her head. "Honey, a half scholarship means you'd still have to pay thousands of dollars. Our Redmond shop is struggling, so we don't have that kind of money, and we don't want you taking out a student loan. Let's wait and see. Other schools have been in touch. There's a very good chance one will come through with a full scholarship."

Amelia's face falls. "But if I don't commit, he'll give the scholarship to someone else, and I'll end up with nothing."

Dad takes a deep breath and exhales. "That's not going to happen. You're a top player and a top student. And we're not asking you to say no. Just tell him you want to wait a little longer before committing. He'll understand."

Amelia's eyes fill with tears as she turns and rushes upstairs to her room. I'm headed to my own room when Mom's voice stops me. "Go talk to her," she says.

"Me? She doesn't want to talk to me."

"Maybe. Maybe not. Give her a chance. It'd be good for her to talk to someone."

I climb the stairs, walk down the hallway, and poke my head inside Amelia's half-open door.

"What?" she says, anger in her voice.

"Nothing. I don't know. I thought you might want to—"

"Just leave me alone. That's all I want."

I start to leave but turn back. "They're right, you know," I say. "Mom and Dad. Those coaches would be crazy not to want you on their team. You're fast, you play smart, you're a good teammate, you won't flunk out. You've got it all."

She looks up. "You really think so?"

"I know it."

The next day, I return to Dr. Charles for what I hope will be my final visit. I haven't had a headache for over a week, and I've started listening to my tunes and playing video games.

Dr. Charles runs tests checking my reaction times and my memory. "You're good to go, Nate," he says when the exam is over. "If you feel any symptoms, come back to see me. Don't be a macho idiot. You've only got one brain."

"Perfect timing," my dad says in the car going home. "You'll be one hundred percent for soccer season."

I don't say anything to him, figuring it's better to wait and tell both him and Mom at the same time that I'm quitting. I do get a pit in my stomach, though, as I think about the argument that's coming.

Mom's car is in the driveway when we reach home. Dad parks next to it. I get out, and as I head toward the house, I take a deep breath to suck in some courage. No point in waiting—as soon as I step inside, I'll break the news and face the blowback.

I never get the chance. Before my dad reaches the porch, the front door bursts open and Amelia rushes out, beaming. "I got it. A full scholarship to Cal Berkeley. Coach Nguyen said he couldn't risk losing me to another school. I'm in!"

Mom is standing just behind Amelia—her face glowing. Dad picks Amelia up and swings her around. When he puts her down, Amelia hugs me. "Thanks for saying what you said," she whispers.

19

YOU GET YOURSELF PUMPED TO do something at a certain moment, and that moment goes by and the whole thing fizzles. At least that is how it is for me. That night we eat at the Monkey Bridge, a Vietnamese restaurant that's Amelia's favorite. She brings up pictures of the Cal campus on her phone, and we take turns looking at them. It's not the right time for me to say anything. I tell myself to let a few days go by, but the few days turn into a week, and then it's Christmas break, and Christmas break means Grandfather and Grandmother Frick.

For four days it's boring family time. We go to Zoolights at the Point Defiance Zoo in Tacoma and to *A Christmas Carol* at ACT. Over and over, my grandparents embarrass Amelia, pumping her for details on her soccer exploits and her school achievements, oohing and aahing the whole time. My mom and dad try to squeeze me into the conversation, but what is there to say?

On Christmas Day, Grandfather Frick gives me a card with

one hundred dollars inside. From the expression on Amelia's face I can tell that she got a lot more. Grandmother Frick leans toward me and whispers, "Don't worry, Nate, if you go to college, we'll do the same for you."

For Christmas dinner, Mom bakes a turkey, with stuffing and gravy; Dad does the salads and the mashed potatoes. "I thought we'd have submarine sandwiches," Grandfather Frick says when we sit down, and then he laughs, though nobody else thinks it's funny, except Grandmother Frick, who only half hides her smile. All through dinner Grandfather Frick talks about Seattle being full of homeless people and drug addicts. "I don't know how you live here; I really don't." He must say that five times. The next morning, my mom sighs in relief when the taxi drives off, taking them to Sea-Tac for the flight to Missoula.

20

WITH MY GRANDPARENTS GONE, IT'S the perfect time for me to make my stand against playing soccer, but I don't. Instead, for the rest of Christmas break and for the first couple of weeks of January, I let one day slide into the next.

Just before the MLK holiday, an announcement comes over the intercom reminding anyone interested in a spring sport to get their medical forms in by the end of the week.

"Have you turned in your paperwork?" Amelia asks me that night at dinner just as I shove a forkful of spaghetti into my mouth.

I shake my head as the blood rushes to my face.

"They're due Friday, Nate," she says. "You heard Ms. Clyburn's announcement, right?"

"What paperwork?" Dad asks. "What are we talking about here?"

"Soccer," Amelia says when I stay quiet.

Now it's Mom's turn. "Where are the forms, Nate? You've had a physical, but we'll probably need to get a signature from someone in Dr. Charles's office."

"You don't need to fill anything out," I say. "I'm not going to play soccer."

My parents exchange a look of surprise.

"What do you mean you're not playing?" Mom asks.

"Just what I said," I answer, trying to keep my voice from shaking. "I'm not playing."

Dad leans back. "Because of the concussion? That was a fluke, Nate. Besides, you don't want fear to keep you from the things you love."

"I don't love soccer," I say. "You and Mom and Amelia love soccer. I hate soccer."

Mom gives me a little smile. "Nate, that's not true. We've seen you play; we know you enjoy it."

"I don't enjoy it," I say, "at least not anymore. I suck in the field and I'm just okay at goalie." I look first at my dad, then at my mom, finally at Amelia. "You know it's true."

There's a long silence. "It's fine if you don't play soccer," Mom says. "But your dad and I want you to play something. Tennis, track, golf, Ultimate Frisbee—it doesn't matter. We just want you active, doing positive things with people your own age." She pauses. "Okay?"

"I want to play basketball," I say, and then I plunge ahead before anyone can stop me. "I think I can be good, way better than I'd ever be at soccer. Maybe even as good as Colin Vatonen by the time I'm a senior."

When I finish, Amelia stares at me as if I'm a loon. "You're joking, right?" she says. "I mean, you haven't played on any basketball team at any level. Ever. You can't seriously think you're—"

"Amelia!" Mom snaps.

"Well, he acts like he can shoot around for ten minutes and—"

"Amelia!" This time it's Dad. "Enough!"

More silence.

Finally, Mom speaks, her voice calm. "Basketball is a great choice, Nate. If I hadn't played soccer, that would've been my game." She raises her hands to her eyes and shoots at an imaginary basket by the sink. "I could always fill it up."

My dad winds some noodles around his fork. "Let's hope you get your mom's talent," he says, "because the basketball and I were never friends."

Upstairs in my room after dinner, I can hear my parents talking in the kitchen. Amelia is in her bedroom, door closed, listening to Mozart or Beethoven or somebody like that, which she started doing once she got the scholarship to Cal.

I slip halfway down the stairs, where they can't see me, but I can hear them. It's Mom's voice I pick up first. "Do you think he has any chance?"

Dad snickers softly. "Amelia's right. The kids he'll be up against have been playing basketball for years. Does he even know the rules?"

"So what do we do?" Mom says.

Dad sighs. "The rec department runs a spring league that

43

has a no-cut policy. We'll sign him up for that. The other players will be basketball wannabes like him. He'll fit in, and hopefully, he'll be satisfied."

Mom laughs softly. "One good thing. No more standing in the rain watching him warm the bench."

"Come on," Dad says. "He played some."

"Not much," Mom says, laughing. "And admit it. His playing time wasn't much more exciting than his bench time."

A chair squeaks as one of them stands. I slink back to my room, an ache in my gut. They'd always told me they liked watching my games, and I'd been stupid enough to believe them.

That ache in my gut morphs into anger. They think my basketball plan is idiotic. Fine. I'll show them.

21

MY BIRTHDAY IS ON FEBRUARY eighth. "Anything special you want?" my dad asks the Saturday before.

When I tell him, he grimaces. "I don't want to pound nails into the siding, but I'll figure out something."

And he does. When I come home from school on my birthday, in a big box on the driveway is a Spalding Pro Slam hoop with a plexiglass backboard.

It has a wheeled base, but once we set it up in our driveway, I never move it. My dad is worried that it might topple over, so I go with him to Stoneway Hardware, where we buy six fifty-pound bags of sand. Back home, we put those on top of the base for stability. Even then he's concerned. "Don't ever hang on the rim. If this topples over, it could kill you, and I'm not joking."

Amelia gives me a black-and-green Spalding indoor/outdoor basketball that feels like a leather ball even though it isn't. Inside her birthday card are the words "Go Bro!" At the very bottom, in smaller letters, is the single word: "Sorry."

We go to Katsu Burger for dinner, so I can't shoot around on my new hoop until Saturday morning. The people who lived in our house before us had cemented over a big chunk of the front yard for their boat. My parents turned it into a patio, putting potted trees and plants out there, along with some Adirondack chairs. By sliding the pots and chairs off to the side, I create a decent court.

I've been shooting for about thirty minutes, getting the feel for the hoop and the ball, when my mom, wearing sweats, tennis shoes, and a Seahawks headband, comes out. "Okay if I play?" she says.

"Sure," I say, though I'm still feeling the sting from her and my dad laughing at me.

Once she's loose, she challenges me to a game of HORSE, and she crushes me three times in a row. Then we go one-on-one, and she beats me again. That's how she is, and my dad too. When I was little, they treated Chutes and Ladders as if it were an Olympic event.

"That was fun," she says as she heads back into the house. "We'll have to do it again." Fun for her, but for me a slap in the face. A light rain starts to fall. I start to head inside, but then return to the court. If I'm going to get good at this game, I can't let a few drops of water stop me.

22

EVERY DAY AFTER SCHOOL AND for hours on Saturday and Sunday I wear out the driveway shooting hoops, playing imaginary games, fantasizing about winning the NBA title with a deep three or a driving lay-in at the buzzer.

While I'm shooting at my hoop, Lucas is standing by the curb waiting for Megan's bus. When it pulls up, they go inside for ten minutes or so. Then they come out and shoot around at the crooked hoop Bill nailed to the willow tree.

The whole thing is weird. We're fifty feet apart, playing the same game, and we each act as if the other guy doesn't exist. Sometimes I catch Lucas looking over at me, and sometimes he catches me looking at him. Playing alone is okay, but you can pretend to beat LeBron only so many times. I need a flesh-and-blood opponent.

One day I clank a three-pointer off the back iron so badly that the ball bounces past me and out into the street, toward Lucas.

I chase it down and pick it up, and our eyes meet. "You want to shoot some on my hoop?" I ask.

"Okay if Megan comes over, too?" he says.

"Sure," I say. "No problem."

We shoot around for a while, all three of us, before he challenges me to a game. "What about Megan?" I ask. "What's she going to do?"

He moves over to her; they talk quietly; he returns. "She'll keep score. So don't say it out loud."

I was confused. "What do you mean?" I ask.

"I mean Megan will say the score out loud," he says. "Nobody else. Game to eleven, count by ones, win by one. Okay?"

From the start, we go hard at each other. *No blood; no foul.* I've heard that expression, but I've never played it. At Salmon Bay, Colin Vatonen and Bo Dietz whine over the smallest taps on the arm. Neither Cawley nor I foul on purpose, but if it happens . . . play on. Whenever either of us scores, Megan's voice rings out. *"Lucas six; Nate three."* She never makes a mistake, not that day or any day.

When we played before, I won at least half the games, and probably more. Now I've been practicing on a better hoop with a better ball. I have Nike shoes and a Nike jersey and Nike shorts, while everything Lucas has looks like it was rejected by Goodwill. I'm certain I'll win way more than half.

Wrong.

He crushes me 11–7, 11–5, 11–7, and I have to fight to make the games that close. Most guys get ahead and start jacking up shots from outside, looking for easy hoops, but not Lucas. He backs me down time after time and then rises for a short jump shot. If he misses, he goes after the rebound like a wildcat.

After the third game, I turn on the spigot and we take turns gulping water from the hose. When we return to the court, it's Megan's turn. She shoots a few from straightaway and from the corners. Then she bounces the ball hard against the pavement and watches with joy as it rises against the sky. If it bounds away, there are two of us to chase it down. She is still bouncing the ball when a Domino's delivery guy pulls up in front of their house.

23

WE PLAY AGAIN THE NEXT day, and most days after that. Sometimes my mom or dad comes home while we're still playing. They never say anything, but I get a *be careful* look each time. Lucas Cawley is not the friend they want me to have.

The routine never changes. Lucas and I go at it one-on-one for forty-five minutes or so, with Megan keeping score. He is stronger and has a hunger for the ball, but I'm developing my shooting touch. I'll get the ball up in my fingertips, picture the perfect arc, release. When my shot is in sync, I'll win. If my shot is off, he'll grind me down with hard drives to the hoop and aggressive rebounding. After three games, it's Megan's turn.

At dinner one night, there is talk all around me, but I'm not paying attention. Amelia asks me a question that I don't answer. She waves her hand in front of me. "Earth to Nate," she says. "Come in, please."

I shrug. "Sorry."

Mom looks at me. "What's up?"

"Nothing."

"Come on, Nate. Something's bothering you. What is it?"

"I was just thinking about Megan Cawley."

"Megan Cawley?" Amelia scoffs in disbelief. "Since when did you care about Megan Cawley?"

"I see her every day," I shoot back.

Amelia is about to say more, but my dad puts his hand up, and she stops.

"What about Megan Cawley?" he asks.

"Forget it," I say, glaring at Amelia.

"No," Dad says. "I want to hear."

"What's going to happen to her once Lucas moves out? He can't take care of her his whole life."

My parents exchange a look. "She has her parents," Mom says. "That won't change."

"But they're no good now, and they won't get better when they get older. Lucas gets her on and off the bus; he checks her backpack and all that. Anyway, eventually the parents will die, so then what happens to her?"

Amelia's eyes widen. "Wow! You really have been—"

"Amelia," Mom says sharply, and she stops.

Mom turns to me. When she speaks, her voice is precise. "The state takes care of people with special needs, people like Megan. It's not great care, but it's not terrible care, either. When the time comes, she'll move into a group home."

"So she won't end up homeless?"

"No, no," Dad says. "That won't happen."

That night, as I'm getting ready for bed, I hear a basketball bouncing on the street and push the curtains aside on the window that looks out across the street. It's a cold, windy, rainy night, but Lucas is there, alone in the moonlight, shooting at his crooked hoop.

24

IN THE PAST, AT LUNCH during basketball season, I only half listened as Colin and Bo and other guys talked about their games. I wasn't thinking of myself as a basketball player then. I'd paid enough attention to know that the JV team had done okay, even though—according to Colin—their coach, Mr. Rodriguez, sucked. I also knew that at the end of the season, Colin and Bo had been promoted to varsity and had started the last four games, three of them victories.

With the season over, those two brag about their Champions Hoops Academy team. The coach is great; the competition is great; the facilities are great.

As they talk, the truth comes rushing in. Playing against Lucas Cawley is better than having no competition, but it's nothing like having a real coach who runs real workouts. Amelia plays year-round on select teams—that's how she got so good.

X X X

That night, after I finish my homework, I print the application form for Champions Academy and go downstairs to talk to my parents. They are both at the kitchen table, spreadsheets all around them.

"What's up?" my dad says when I appear in the doorway.

"If you're busy, I can—"

"No," my mom says. "We're wrapping this up. What's on your mind?"

I plunge into a full description of the Champions Hoops Academy and how much I would learn if I joined. "I need to do this," I say, finishing. "It's the only way I can catch up."

I push the forms toward them. My dad picks them up and scans them, with my mom leaning close so she can read them too. He stops at the last page and points. "Nate, this is quite a bit of money."

I'm ready for that. "Amelia is on a select team. You pay for her."

My dad shakes his head. "Not the same, bud."

"How is it different?" I ask, angry.

Mom tries to pat my hand, but I pull away. "Nate," she says, "Amelia has dedicated herself to soccer for ten years."

I shrug. "Yeah. Okay. So?"

"So, we didn't sign her up for select soccer the first time she kicked a ball." She pauses. "Look, we're glad you're interested in basketball, but your interest isn't even two months old and you want to go straight to an expensive AAU club?" She shakes her head. "That's too big an ask."

"I'm not worth it. That's what you're saying."

"Don't even start that," my dad says, an edge to his voice. "You know that's not true. You're done with soccer; you want to play basketball. We get it. Play on the rec team, see how you like it, see how you do." He opens his hand toward the papers on the table. "You show a real commitment to basketball, we'll talk again down the road. Fair?"

I can feel the blood pulsing in my head. "Whatever," I say as I grab the application form off the table and tromp back upstairs.

For about an hour I think about quitting basketball, but I know that would prove my parents and Amelia right. So instead I fill out the rec league registration papers.

When I bring the papers downstairs the next morning, my mom signs at the bottom and writes me a check for twenty dollars. I take it and mutter my thanks. Before I can get away, she points out the window toward the Cawley house.

"What about Lucas?" she asks.

"What about him?" I say.

Mom's eyebrows go up. "He's been your partner, right? Maybe he'd want to play on the rec team."

My body tenses. It's okay to play against Lucas in the driveway where no one will see us, but to walk into a gym with Creepy Crawley?

That's what flashes through my mind, but it's not what I tell my mom. "He can't," I say. "He's got to watch Megan."

"She's got a father and a mother," Mom says. "Lucas can leave her for a couple of hours." She pauses. "At least ask him. And don't mention the money. We'll pay it."

I nod, but when we go one-on-one that afternoon, I never bring up the rec league.

"He said he couldn't," I tell my mom that night, and she shrugs.

"You tried."

25

MY FIRST REC TEAM PRACTICE is Tuesday night at Loyal Heights Community Center, which is just a few blocks away. Although I arrive ten minutes early, other guys are already shooting around. I figure our coach will be somebody's dad, but he turns out to be Ethan Chan, a senior at Shilshole High who'd played varsity.

"Call me Coach C," he says before he has us do some basic passing drills. After that, we run lines, do more passing drills, run more lines, and then break into groups to shoot at side hoops. Everything we do, he does, really pushing himself. It feels more like a workout class than a basketball practice.

Practice starts at seven thirty. At exactly eight thirty, Coach C blows his whistle. "That's it! See you Thursday."

When I step inside the front door at home, Amelia is sprawled out on the sofa, her laptop open. In the kitchen my parents have spreadsheets in front of them. I head straight for my room, but they intercept me.

"How'd it go?" Dad asks.

I give a general report. When I mention Ethan Chan, Amelia sits up. "That is so Ethan," she says in a mocking voice, but smiling. "I heard he still needs community service hours to graduate. He kept putting it off and putting it off. Now he's stuck."

Mom frowns. "Isn't it possible he just wants to do something for others?"

Amelia scoffs. "Mom, everything everybody does is about graduating from high school or getting into college. Besides, no one would mistake Ethan for Mother Teresa, or Father Teresa, if there is such a person. Ethan is all about Ethan."

I think about her comment all through our second practice. Three guys had dropped out, which was no surprise, since that first practice hadn't exactly been thrilling, leaving only nine players—a bad number. Again, Coach C shows up right at seven thirty. Most of the practice is taken up with stretching and running, which he does with us again. No doubt about it—he's using the team practice to get in his own workout.

With twenty minutes left, he breaks us into teams and tells us to scrimmage. "Shouldn't we learn some plays?" asks Nicholas Putnam, a dark-haired kid with superlong arms. "And what about defense?"

Coach C scrunches up his face. "On offense, shoot when you're open, pass when you're not, and move to an empty space if you don't have the ball. On defense, look for the nearest guy nobody is guarding and guard him. If you run into a screener, try to get by him. If you can't get by, switch. Okay?"

I'm pumped as I take the court, eager to prove that I'm going to be THE MAN on our team. Silky-smooth outside shot, solid ballhandling, good defense—no one will match me. When Coach blows a whistle to start the scrimmage, I expect everybody to go into beast mode, to play with the fire that I always need when I play against Lucas.

It doesn't happen. Nobody contests my dribble; nobody tries to rip rebounds out of my hands; nobody sticks their hand in my face when I go up for a jumper. You'd think that would make things easy, but since the other guys aren't doing any of those things, I turn down the volume on my game.

I play decent defense, grab a few rebounds, score a few points. My team is up by two points when Coach C calls out, "Last possession."

They have the ball. Andres Gómez, the guy I'm guarding, dribbles into forecourt. I think about pressuring him, but instead I back off, playing loose. He steps into a three-pointer from the top of the key. Perfect spin, perfect arc, perfect swish.

Gómez's teammates whoop it up before we all head to the exit. Coach C stops me as I reach the door. I'm expecting him to chew me out for my soft defense, but it isn't that at all.

"Has Amelia talked about the senior prom?"

"The senior prom?" I answer, confused.

"I mean, does she have a date?"

"I don't know," I say.

"Could you find out? Only don't tell her I'm asking."

"I can try."

He puts out his fist for me to bump. "That'd be great if you could."

26

IT'S A LONG WALK HOME. I was a mediocre soccer player, and I'm a mediocre basketball player. Ethan Chan didn't chew me out for playing soft defense against Gómez. Mediocre is what he expects. Why else would I be playing rec ball? Making JV as a junior, varsity as a senior? Amelia was right to laugh.

Later, sprawled out on my bed, I think about Lucas. If you have the ball, he's up in your face, and good luck to you if you aren't ready, because he's coming at you like a Muhammad Ali right cross. Why didn't I tell him about the rec league? So what if the other guys call him Creepy Crawley? Caring about stuff like that is just a different way of being soft.

"I'm playing on a team at Loyal Heights Community Center," I say to him the next afternoon while we warm up. "We have uniforms, a clock, referees—the whole thing. Some guys quit, so there's room on the team. The next practice is tomorrow night at seven thirty. The two of us together—we could roll."

His eyes shift toward Megan.

I shrug. "Megan could come watch. Or she could go to the TV room or maybe do an art project or something."

I'm rambling, and I know it, so I stop.

When I step outside my front door the next night, he's across the street, waiting.

"Megan coming?" I ask.

"No," he says.

I'm afraid Ethan Chan will tell Lucas he needs to fill out a bunch of forms at the main desk, but that doesn't happen. "Glad to have another warm body," Coach C says, giving Lucas a fist bump. "You ever play on a team before?"

Lucas shakes his head.

Coach C laughs. "Don't worry about it. I don't think anybody else has either. Get out there and warm up. I need to talk to Nathan here for a second.

"Amelia?" he says once Lucas is out of earshot. "You find out anything?"

"Sort of."

"So, tell me."

"My mom says that Amelia hasn't mentioned the prom, so that probably means—"

"Yeah, yeah," Coach C says. "I get what it means." He pauses. "When we were little, I called her Amelia Bedelia. Do you think she remembers?"

"Probably," I say, "but lots of kids called her that."

× × ×

The first half of that practice is like the others—Coach C getting in his workout, the rest of us following along. Eventually he lets us scrimmage.

About half the players are Salmon Bay K–8 guys, so they know Lucas as Creepy Crawley. That makes it easy to work it so that Lucas and I are both on the Green team. The Red team wins the tip, and instantly Lucas goes after his guy like a dog goes after a cat, swiping at the ball and slapping it free. It bounces toward me; I snatch it as he streaks toward our hoop. A simple pass leads to an easy lay-in, and we are off. He plays defense like a pit bull, and the rest of us follow his lead, elevating our effort. Defense leads to open looks on offense. I hit three of six from long range and we jump out to a 14–6 lead.

We keep the pressure on, and the guys on the Red team start whining. "That was a charge," Dustin Long, a tall, red-haired kid with a long, thin face, shouts at Coach C after Lucas plows over him on the way to the hoop.

Coach C scoffs. "Suck it up, Dustin." That's the phrase he uses over and over. We win 38–21. I score fifteen, Lucas ten, and Bryan Alfara—who'd done nothing in any of the earlier scrimmages—hustles his way to eight points and a bunch of rebounds.

Lucas and I are leaving when Coach C calls us back. "That was great, what you two did to the Red team." He punches me lightly on the shoulder. "Where you been hiding that intensity? You channel your sister today?"

"I don't know," I say, wishing he'd stop mentioning Amelia.

He rubs his hands together. "All right, so here's the situation.

First game is Thursday, against Crown Hill. This is a rec league—so everybody plays at least one quarter of the game. I'm going to start Gómez at guard along with that kid with the goggles. What's his name?"

"Alex Kovar," I say.

"Right," he says. "Kovar. They'll play the way they play, lulling Crown Hill into thinking we're one kind of team. Then, in the second quarter, I'll put you two in. You smack them around on defense and make them pay for turnovers."

That night I tell my parents about Lucas joining the team. "That's great," my mom says. She pauses. "We'd still be glad to pay."

I tell them that Ethan Chan didn't mention anything about paying or even have Lucas fill out the registration.

"Perfect Ethan," Amelia says.

27

IT'S A REC LEAGUE, THE teams filled with guys who either got cut from their school teams or didn't try out. Still, on the night of our first game, I'm pacing around after dinner like a panther stuck in a cage. When it's time for me to leave, my mom says that she and my dad want to see the game.

I wave her off. "No parents are going to be there," I say. "It'd be weird if you showed up—"

"You sure?" my dad pipes in. "I always like watching a game."

"I'm sure," I say, my hand turning the doorknob.

Outside, Lucas and Megan are shooting at the crooked hoop. When he sees me, he takes her hand and walks her to the back door of their house. It opens; they both step inside; the door closes. I wait. A minute . . . two minutes . . . three . . . My stomach churns. The door opens, and Lucas steps out. "Let's go," he says.

Inside the gym, Coach C hands each of us an old green

T-shirt with the words LOYAL HEIGHTS LIONS written in yellow across the front. I'm number 5; Lucas is 11. We yank off our shirts and pull those on.

The Crown Hill Cobras' gym is a mile away. We pile into the Loyal Heights van, which Bryan Alfara's father drives. "We'll be there in five minutes," he says. "So don't anybody start singing 'John Jacob Jingleheimer Schmidt.'" Bryan rolls his eyes and shakes his head.

Coach C keeps Lucas and me on the bench to start the game. The first quarter is weirdly gentle, as if it's a demonstration video on YouTube. Our guards, Gómez and Kovar, bring the ball up and pass it around until somebody takes a shot or turns it over. Then the Cobras do the same. Rebounds aren't contested; passing lanes are open. Even guys driving to the hoop are given free passage. When the quarter ends, the Cobras lead 12–8 and the refs haven't called a single foul, because there haven't been any.

Coach C subs Lucas and me in to start the second quarter. "*Beast mode,*" he says, a wicked gleam in his eye.

We don't let him down. Lucas jumps the passing lanes, traps guys in corners, crashes the boards, and I'm right there with him, or maybe a half step behind. Whenever we force a turnover, we're off on a fast break. Sometimes he takes it to the hole; sometimes I spot up for an open look. Putnam, Long, and Alfara chip in with putbacks and rebounds.

Lucas gets his first foul—over the back—two minutes into the quarter. He gets his second—an ugly tripping foul that brings the Cobras' coach howling off the bench—a minute later. The calls don't slow Lucas down. I wonder, *Does he know about fouling out?*

The Cobras are on the ropes; their 12–8 lead has turned into a 22–16 deficit. In the final minute before halftime, Lucas slaps the ball loose from their point guard, grabs it, and races downcourt. They have a guy back on defense, so Lucas kicks the ball out to me. I gather myself and release a high, arcing shot. Swish!

Coach C's eyes are lit up. "That was great," he says during halftime. He makes a fist. "Pedal to the metal until the final buzzer. Let's win by fifty."

I hope Lucas and I will start the second half, but it's Gómez and Kovar again. This time, though, they play with grit. Not Lucas-tough, but tougher than they'd been. At the end of three, our lead is 36–21.

When the Cobras see Lucas and me heading onto the court at the beginning of the fourth quarter, their faces go ashen. We stick a fork in them, scoring six straight on a couple of driving lay-ins by Lucas followed by a Putnam jumper from the free throw line. Coach C puts his hands, palm down, in front of his waist, signaling we should back off, but Lucas has no back-off in him.

We're up by twenty-eight, with less than a minute left, when one of their guys slaps the ball away from me and lopes downcourt for a breakaway hoop. He takes it too easy, though. Lucas catches him, goes up, and blocks the shot, sending the kid crashing to the floor. The Cobras' coach jumps to his feet. "That's a flagrant foul!" he screams to the ref before wheeling around to face Coach C. "What kind of team are you coaching? Look at the score!"

"Sorry! Sorry!" Coach C calls back, and he yanks Lucas out of the game. Once his back is turned to the Cobras' coach, Coach C gives Lucas a thumbs-up and a smile.

When I get home, I take a shower and pull on some sweats. I'm headed back to my room when Amelia's door opens.

"Did you win?" she asks.

"Yeah, we scorched them."

"Great. Good for you." She pauses. "Did Ethan tell you that I'm going with him to the senior prom?"

28

THAT FIRST GAME SETS THE tone for the season. The refs want to get the games over with, so they don't call many fouls, which works to our advantage, since Lucas intimidates everybody both with his play and the crazy look in his eyes. Nobody would guess that before every game he takes Megan's hand and leads her back into their house. We win and win and win.

During lunch, I listen to Colin and Bo describe their games. I burn to say something about my team, but a rec team is nothing compared with an AAU team.

With one game left in the season, we are tied for first with a 10–1 record. Our one loss had been to the West Woodland Wolves at their gym, and it was a cheap loss. Only seven West Woodland players suited up for that game, and all were good. While Lucas and I were on the bench because of the league rule about playing time, they were able to pile up the points against our weak players.

The last game is the rematch, on Thursday night, this time

at our gym. The Wolves had also lost once, so the winner will take the league title.

Throughout the season I've told my mom and dad that no parents are at the games. "There's no place to sit," I say. "In fact, there's hardly any place to stand." It's a lie—about a dozen parents are at every game.

Now I'm so pumped with the thought of winning a title that I'm going to ask my parents and Amelia to come to Thursday's game. But before school on Wednesday morning, Amelia's cell chimes.

She says hello, and her voice grows excited. She turns and looks at us, eyes wide. "Yes," she says. "Yes. . . . Definitely. . . . Yes. . . . That would be great. . . . They're both right here. I'll ask right now."

She cuts the volume on the phone. "It's Coach Nguyen from Cal. He's in Seattle and wants to have dinner with all of us tomorrow night. We can do it, right?"

"Of course we can," Dad says. "We'll take him to Ray's Boathouse."

She turns the volume back up on her phone and arranges the details. When she disconnects, she turns to me. "You're invited, too," she says.

I shake my head. "I've got a game."

Amelia looks disappointed, which surprises me.

"Any chance you could skip it?" my dad asks.

I feel my face flush with anger. They'd never ask Amelia to miss a game. "No," I say.

"At least think about it," my mom says. "It could be a family celebration."

"I don't need to think about it," I say. "I've got a game."

My dad puts up his hands. "Fine, fine. No need to get huffy. We just want you to know you're invited."

29

AFTER MY PARENTS AND AMELIA leave on Thursday night, I microwave a burrito, eat half of it, watch YouTube videos for twenty minutes, and then head out to meet Lucas. He's standing alone on the sidewalk, and he tells me to go without him.

I panic. "But you're going to be there, right?"

"Yeah, I'll be there."

Coach C has the same fear when he sees me alone. He opens his hands. "Where's Lucas?"

"He's coming," I say.

As we warm up, I keep looking over to the entrance. So does Coach C. So does every guy on the team.

Where is he?

A few minutes before game-time, the door swings open and Lucas walks in, Bill and Megan behind him. He leads them to folding chairs set up in a corner and gets them settled. As he turns to join us, Megan claps.

Instead of starting Gómez and Kovar, Coach C puts Lucas

and me out there. His idea is to open fast, but the change throws us off. West Woodland jumps to a 4–0 lead after Lucas turns the ball over on our first possession and Putnam throws the ball away on our second.

We settle in and play our brand of basketball, suffocating their offense, forcing turnovers or wild shots. Lucas gets a put-back, muscling a guy four inches taller out of the way, to give us our first lead at 9–8, and when Dustin Long gets a three-point play just before the end of the quarter, our lead is 14–10.

Once Gómez and Kovar take our spots, though, the Wolves whittle away at our lead. The score is 16–15 midway through the quarter. Then the Wolves go up 21–18 with a couple of minutes left before halftime. Coach C calls a time-out to break the flow, but it doesn't work. At the half we're down 26–20.

"Don't try to get it all back at once," Coach C says during the break. "Let the game come to you. No panic."

Easier to say than to do.

At the start of the second half, West Woodland's point guard brings the ball into the forecourt and makes a simple pass to the wing. Lucas breaks on it, trying for a steal, bumping the guy. All season, refs had let ticky-tack fouls go, but this time I hear the whistle—number three on Lucas.

After a couple of empty possessions for both sides, we score on a jumper by Dustin Long. Lucas picks up their point guard at half-court, trying to pick his pocket as he dribbles.

Another light bump.

Another whistle.

Foul number four.

Coach C calls time. As we circle around him, I see him stare at the scoreboard. He looks at Lucas. Let him play and risk him fouling out? Take him out and risk West Woodland burying us?

He turns to Lucas. "Back off for the rest of this quarter. You hear me? No fouls. Then go beast mode in the fourth."

As we return to the court, my eyes fall on Megan. She's clapping and smiling, her eyes alive. Bill, too, looks like a different person. He's sitting straight and tall, his chin up, his eyes fixed on Lucas. "You can do it!" he's shouting. "You can do it!"

We drift through the rest of the third quarter, Lucas protecting himself by playing soft, which must have killed him. I hit a couple of outside shots to keep the game within reach; still, when the horn sounds ending the third, West Woodland leads 36–28.

"Title on the line," Coach C says as we huddle before the fourth quarter. "Maximum effort."

Lucas is like a thoroughbred that has been held back until reaching the stretch. Now—finally—he can go. A minute into the quarter he makes a steal, followed by a perfect pass to me for a lay-in. On the next Wolves' possession, he snares a rebound, makes a quick outlet pass. I drive toward the hoop, then dish off to Dustin Long, and we have a second lay-in.

As the remaining minutes of the game tick away, the refs swallow their whistles, letting us play. Lucas gets right up in the face of the guy he's guarding, so we all do. With three minutes left, we're down by three. With ninety seconds left, we lead by one. Then, after all that work to get the lead, West Woodland catches us sleeping with a backdoor play that leads to an easy bucket, putting them back on top.

Nerves hit both sides. I try a stupid bullet pass to Putnam, who has posted up. He's open, but my pass is so hard that an NFL receiver would have had trouble hanging on. The ball goes through his hands and off the back wall. Turnover.

The Wolves, ahead by one, run some clock before their point guard comes off a screen for a three-pointer from the top of the key. It's on-line, but a foot short. Airball.

Back to us.

Twenty-two seconds left.

I bring the ball up and hit Putnam in the corner—another stupid pass. They trap him, and I think he'll turn the ball over, but he manages to get a bounce pass back to me.

Eleven seconds.

Lucas sets a screen that I use to rub my guy off. I rise for the winning shot.

It feels perfect, but with the extra adrenaline, it's too strong. I'm sure we've lost, but Lucas muscles through two guys to snatch the rebound. He goes right back up, fights through the contact, and gets the ball on the rim. It hangs there, teetering, and falls in.

We're back up by one.

Five seconds on the clock. West Woodland inbounds quickly. I harass my guy, waving my arms around but careful not to foul. He makes a long pass that Putnam picks off. He dribbles once, the horn sounds, and he flings the ball high in the air.

We are the champions!

30

AFTER SHAKING HANDS WITH THE West Woodland guys, we follow Coach C to a meeting room, laughing and punching one another the whole way. On a table in front of the room is a cake decorated to look like a basketball court. Next to the cake are a bunch of cheap plastic trophies and one large trophy with the letters MVP across the pedestal in the front.

I look around for Lucas. Where is he? Then I spot him, with Megan and Bill, heading for the gym door. Our eyes meet. I give him a little head nod to say *Come on back here*, but he keeps walking.

Lots of parents are there. Gómez's mother—she seems to have organized it all—cuts the cake and puts slices on paper plates. One of the dads hands each of us a fork and a napkin. On another table are plastic cups in front of two-liter bottles of Coke and Sprite. Within a minute we're stuffing cake into our mouths and gulping down soda.

As we gorge, Coach C calls our names, and guys troop up

to get the little plastic trophies. Player after player is called, and still I sit. My heart is thumping so hard it feels about to explode out of my chest. Finally, I'm the only player left. Is the MVP trophy really mine? It would be fantastic to tell my parents and Amelia that we'd won the title and then show them my MVP trophy.

Now Coach C is saying my name, but instead of holding out the MVP trophy, he extends the last of the plastic trophies toward me. I take it, thank him, and wobble back to my seat.

Once I'm seated, Coach C clears his throat. "Unfortunately, our MVP was unable to stay, but let's all give Lucas Cawley a big Loyal Heights Lions cheer anyway. He got us roaring."

Of course it's Lucas. It was stupid to think it would be me. Everybody cheers, and I join, swallowing the lump in my throat.

"Nate," Coach C goes on, holding the trophy toward me. "Can you get this to him?"

I finish my cake, shake Coach C's hand, say goodbye to the other players, and leave, the ground swaying beneath my feet.

On the walk home, I look hard at Lucas's trophy. It's made of metal and wood and is nearly a foot high. Before I step into my home, I dump my plastic trophy in the trash.

When I open the door, my mom and dad and Amelia are in the front room, talking excitedly.

"There he is," Dad says as I step inside. "How was your game?"

"It was good," I say.

"Does that mean you won?" Amelia asks. "Ethan was so nervous today."

"Yeah, by a point. Lucas got a putback right before the buzzer."

"How exciting," Mom says. "I wish we could have been there."

"What's that?" Amelia asks.

I look down at Lucas's trophy. "This?"

Before I can explain, Amelia has come over and taken it from me. She reads the inscription, then looks up with a big smile. "You were MVP! Congratulations!" she says as she gives me a fist bump.

Quickly Mom is by my side, and Dad is also moving toward me. "You've been holding out on us," Mom says as she gives me a hug. "I wish you'd have let us come to some of the games."

Dad takes the trophy from Amelia, clears out the center spot on the fireplace mantel, and puts the trophy in the place of honor.

"MVP on a championship team," Dad says. "That's quite an achievement."

My head is spinning; my legs feel like noodles. I want to explain, to say *No, you've got it wrong*, but I don't. "I need to shower," I say instead.

"That's actually a very good idea," Amelia says, taking a step back and making a face.

In the shower, I let the water pour over me, wanting to stay forever. I dry myself, put on some clean sweats, and try to read "Harrison Bergeron," a weird sci-fi story for English class about a world where everybody had to be average. I can't concentrate, so I flick off the light and close my eyes.

Sleep doesn't come. I want to think about the game, relive the plays I'd made, recapture the excitement. All I can think about, though, is that stupid MVP trophy on the mantel.

Around one o'clock I hear Amelia's door open and her footsteps on the stairs. I open my door and listen as she rattles around in the kitchen, probably making some herbal tea. I slip downstairs to join her.

"MVP! MVP!" Amelia whisper-chants when I step into the room.

"Stop," I say.

"Why?" she says as she turns the stove on to boil water. "You should be proud. Ethan says you've been playing great."

"It's not mine," I say, sitting down at the kitchen table.

A look of confusion comes over her face. "What's not yours?"

I explain how everything had gotten balled up. "I'll tell Mom and Dad in the morning," I say. "And then I'll bring the trophy to Lucas."

"I'm sorry I jumped in," Amelia says.

"It's just a screwup. Not your fault."

The water is boiling. She pours it over her tea bag and then looks at me. "You want some?"

"Sure," I say. I hate tea, but it's nice sitting with her. She gets a second tea bag and cup, pours the water. "The Cal coach seem okay?" I ask.

"More than okay. I really liked him. He's very funny." She pauses. "You should come visit me at Berkeley."

"We'll be down there a bunch."

Her face puckers. "I don't mean with Mom and Dad. I mean

just you. They've got a room in the athletic dorm where you could stay. Maybe come during basketball season. We could see the Bears play Stanford. That sound good?"

"That sounds great," I say, surprised by the invitation.

We drink the tea in silence for a few minutes, and then she stands. "I'm beat. I'm going to finish this in my room. See you in the morning." She takes a few steps before turning back. "And I'm really, really sorry."

31

IN THE MORNING, I GATHER my courage as I head downstairs. "I told them," Amelia whispers, meeting me at the bottom of the stairs.

That throws me off. "What? Why?"

"Why?" she says. "Because it was my fault."

Just then Mom comes out of the kitchen, with Dad behind her. "Hey," she says. "It's all squared away. And you're still MVP around here."

They leave me alone as I eat a bowl of Cheerios and a couple pieces of toast. When I finish, I look out the front window. Lucas and Megan are sitting on the curb waiting for Megan's bus. I grab my backpack and the trophy and am out the door.

"You won this," I say, shoving the trophy into Lucas's hands. "Most Valuable Player. Everybody clapped like crazy when Coach C announced it." Before he can reply, I'm off, heading toward Shilshole High, feeling about ten pounds lighter.

I think I'm done with the Loyal Heights Lions and Lucas and

the MVP trophy, but it comes back one more time. At lunch that day Colin—with Hanna next to him—stops at the table where I'm eating. "Hey, Dravus," he says, "I hear your team won the championship last night."

I feel my face go red. How did he know?

"No big deal," I say. "Just rec league."

"I also heard Creepy Crawley was the MVP." He grins. "Watch out, LeBron! Anyway, congratulations."

I smile and go back to eating my lunch, fighting the urge to squash my tuna sub into his face.

32

THAT SUMMER, IT'S ALL AMELIA all the time. Again. She and my mom shop for stuff for her dorm room—towels and clocks and sheets and throw rugs and other things. Sometimes they shop online; sometimes they drive to Alderwood Mall. When Amelia isn't shopping, she's at a soccer clinic or a tournament or practice.

I get a brochure in the mail for a two-week basketball camp in early July at North Central High. A couple days later, another brochure for a camp in late July at Shorewood High is delivered. When I show my dad, he frowns. "These look terrific, but you'd have to take the bus. We can't keep the sub shops going, get your sister all set for Berkeley, and drive you to basketball clinics. Once your sister is at Cal, it'll be your turn. That's a promise."

I go upstairs and log onto the Metro trip planner. If all the connections work, it's forty minutes to North Central and sixty minutes to Shorewood, but if I miss a connection, I'll be standing for half an hour on Aurora Avenue, which is crime central. The basketball camps are two hours long each day, but not really. There will be breaks for snacks and some boring *get to know your fellow campers* activities. Half the guys will probably be like I was at the soccer camps—forced to be there. It makes no sense to spend two hours on the bus for a mediocre basketball camp when I could walk outside and go one-on-one with Lucas.

I work out a training schedule. I start early each morning by logging onto a YouTube stretching program. I think it will be too easy, but the woman on the video is a rubber band. After I'm stretched out, I jog to the Shilshole High track, where I run four miles, but not like a cross-country guy, because that's not how basketball works. Instead, for the first two miles I sprint the straightaways and walk the turns, and then reverse that for the next two miles. Next, I go to the football field and use the chalked yard markers to do five- and ten-yard dashes, concentrating on my first step, trying to make it explosive. I finish by jumping straight up, bringing my knees to my chest to improve my vertical leap.

I'm home around noon. I eat lunch, then lift weights in the garage. I don't push for personal bests; instead, I slowly increase my reps. I want long, lean muscles, not big muscles that would slow me down.

Once I'm done with my weight work, I reward myself with some video game time, usually *NBA 2K*. Then I go outside and shoot around in front of my house. When Lucas is done helping Bill, he and Megan come over.

In July, I start bringing my iPad out with me, and I open some random YouTube basketball drill. Lucas and I watch, and then we practice whatever we've seen. After that, we go at each other one-on-one until we're exhausted. Then it's Megan's turn . . . and the days slide by.

33

ON THE LAST SATURDAY IN July, I go with my parents and Amelia
to Berkeley to get her settled in her dorm. I'd wanted to stay in
Seattle, and then I'd wanted to bring my basketball, but both
ideas got nixed. "We're going to be busy, Nate," Mom says. "No
time for basketball."

Amelia's dorm room, which is bigger than her room at home,
is on the sixth floor. The windows look east toward the Berkeley
Hills. "Sunrises will be great," my dad says, "and foggy days are
wonderful in their own way."

The week before, Amelia had FedExed four boxes to the
dorm. We spend the morning setting up her room. She moves
her desk to this wall and her bed to that wall, then reverses
them, then reverses them back before she's finally happy.

In the afternoon we walk through the campus and the
nearby streets. My parents take turns telling us about the Free
Speech Movement and People's Park and other stuff that I half
listen to. We eat Mexican food and then see a black-and-white

movie at a beat-up theater on Telegraph Avenue. After that, Amelia goes to her dorm while my parents and I go to a Residence Inn, where they take the bedroom and I get the sofa bed in the other room.

Sunday is breakfast, more walking around, lunch with Amelia's assistant coach, followed by a tour of the soccer facilities. After that it's a trip to Target and an early dinner at an Indian restaurant.

Our flight back to Seattle leaves at eight. The trip is supposed to be a celebration, but it doesn't feel that way when we head for the airport. Amelia hugs both Mom and Dad, which she usually doesn't do, and then she hugs me, which she never does. Her eyes are teary, and she looks scared.

"You're going to do great," Mom says, her voice choking up. "You're ready for this."

34

AUGUST . . . WHICH MEANS SWIMMING AT Blue Ridge. The pool
is two miles from my house, all uphill. I decide to ride my
bike to save some time and to work different muscles, so I'm
sweating when I reach it. I lock up my bike, turn around, and
spot Hanna.

I give her a wave before hustling into the locker room to
change. When I come out, she's standing with Colin and Bo, the
three of them laughing about something.

I mill around, feeling stupid, before a whistle blows and
the lesson starts. Arnold Marsh, a freckled college guy, is our
teacher. He doesn't care if we swim fast so long as our form is
good. For every stroke, he has Hanna demonstrate because her
form is perfect.

"You're amazing," I say to her after she swims a couple laps
of butterfly, her arms rising completely above the water, her
dolphin kick propelling her forward in perfect rhythm with her
arms.

"I've taken dance and gymnastics," she says, shrugging. "It transfers."

The lesson is an hour long, but Marsh turns us loose the last fifteen minutes for free swim. I duck my head underwater and swim the width of the pool. When I come up, I'm right next to Hanna. She smiles. "The creature from the black lagoon."

"What?" I say.

"It's a movie. This creature swims underwater, stalking a girl who is totally clueless that he's even there."

My face goes red. "Sorry, I didn't mean to—"

She laughs. "I know you didn't. I was joking."

Right then, from the high diving board, comes a call from Colin. "Clear out down there."

Like him or not—and I don't—the guy is an athlete. He bounces a few times at the end of the diving board and then flings himself up, out, and down, cutting into the water like a knife going through soft butter. He comes up smiling, his eyes fixed on Hanna as he swims over to us.

"Wow!" she says as he nears. "That was awesome. Do you take diving lessons?"

"No," he answers, filling the space I'd stupidly left between her and me. He nods toward Arnold. "Marsh is always after me to join the Spartan Dive Club, but basketball takes all my time."

Hanna says something that I don't hear. Then Bo swims up and grabs hold of the wall on the other side of her. After they all laugh at something else I don't hear, I put my feet against the wall of the pool, push, and swim off, feeling like a little kid chased away by his older brothers.

When the hour is up, I dry myself off, change back into my jeans and a T-shirt, unlock my bike, and start for home. I'm stopped at the light at Holman Road when I hear my name. I turn and look. Colin and Bo are in a Mazda SUV, and again I feel like a little kid. I haven't even signed up for driver's ed, and Colin's got his license.

"We hear you've got a great hoop," Colin says.

"I don't know if it's great, but it's good."

"Okay if we stop and shoot around?"

Here's something about myself I don't understand. I don't like Colin at all, and never have. Bo is okay when he's not with Colin, which is about one time out of ten. I'd known them since first grade, but at school they sometimes look at me as if they don't know who I am. I'd told myself a million times that I didn't want to be friends with either of them anyway. Now, at the thought that they want to come to my house, my face flushes with excitement. "Yeah," I answer in a too-excited voice. "Sure. Of course." I pause. "Do you know where I live?"

"Yeah," Colin says. "We'll meet you there."

Since the ride home is all downhill, they don't beat me by much. "That is a more than decent hoop," Bo says as I'm putting my bike in the garage. "Does the backboard stay steady on bank shots?"

"It moves a fraction," I say, feeling a surge of pride, "but not enough to affect the shot."

I get the basketball Amelia gave me from the garage and pass it to Colin. He spins it a few times in his fingertips. "I like these," he says. "They feel just like leather."

Another surge of pride.

As we shoot around, they talk about their Champions team. After ten minutes Colin suggests a game of Twenty-one, an every-person-for-himself game—about the closest thing to a real game that you can play with three guys.

But there could have been four, because watching from across the street is Lucas. All I have to do is give him a wave and he'll be over, Megan with him. Instead, I ignore him.

For the next hour we play Twenty-one. Colin wins twice; Bo wins once; I never get a sniff.

It's frustrating. Sure, they're better than me, but not *that* much better. I play scared—never running down loose balls, never pulling down contested rebounds—the same dumb way I played on the rec team before Lucas joined.

And it isn't just that once, or just on the court. Day after day, those two guys muscle me out of the way whenever I try to talk to Hanna at swimming. After the swim lesson they stop by my house for an hour or so and push me around on my own court, crushing me in Twenty-one, in HORSE, in whatever we play, acting like they own the place while they do it.

35

AFTER THE LAST THURSDAY OF swim class, Colin and Bo drive to my house and wait for me to bike home. I get my ball out, we shoot around a little, and then it comes. "Twenty-one?" Colin asks.

"I've got a better idea," I say. I turn and shout across the street. "Hey, Lucas, you want to play?"

When I turn back, Bo and Colin are both staring at me.

"Really?" Colin snickers in a low voice. "Creepy Crawley?"

"His name is Cawley," I say, "and with four we can go two-on-two."

He grimaces. "Fine. But he's not going to be my teammate. You and him against us. Game to eleven, score by ones, win by one."

Lucas gets Megan settled off to the side, and then they take the ball out. Colin inbounds to Bo. Immediately Lucas is up in his grill. Bo looks annoyed, as if Lucas is no more than a pesky gnat that he'll easily shoo away. Instead, Lucas smacks down hard on the ball, knocking it free. He grabs it; I break toward the hoop; he hits me with a perfect pass.

Bucket.

Bo and Colin stand, stunned. Adrenaline surges through my body. For two weeks I'd backed down, played scared. But there is no backdown in Lucas. He doesn't know or care that Bo and Colin are on a select AAU team, that Colin's father played pro ball in Europe. He wouldn't have cared if *they* played in the NBA. He's fearless, all the time, and when I'm on the court with him, I am too.

I fire the basketball to Bo. "One–zip," I say.

He catches the ball, stares me down, and then glares at Lucas, a glare that says *All right. You want that kind of game, you got it.*

They dribble better, shoot better, pass better, but we get the loose balls and out-rebound them. There's nothing pretty about our game, yet our effort gives us second-chance shots, and those extra shots keep the game close.

It's tied at eight when Bo sets a high screen for Colin. Colin takes a hard dribble to the right as Bo rolls—unguarded—to the hoop. The pass is right there for the easy layup.

9–8.

On our next possession, Lucas drives and kicks the ball out to me. My shot hits off the back rim. Colin rebounds, brings the ball back, and they go to that same pick-and-roll play. I stay with Bo, but he steps back and banks in a jumper.

10–8.

One more and we're done.

Lucas inbounds. I eye the hoop, feel good, go up. Just as I'm rising, Lucas cuts back door. I turn my shot into a pass that he catches in stride and lays in.

10–9.

They still need only one hoop to win. I'm expecting the same pick-and-roll, so I sag off, daring Colin to shoot. He lets the ball go. Nice arc, perfect spin, but the shot hits the front rim, short. Lucas snatches the rebound, whips a pass to me in the corner, and up I go, as free as a bird.

Swish!

10–10.

Next basket wins.

Bo inbounds to Colin, and I'm up on him. Colin's eyes shift to Bo, waiting for him to break free from Lucas. When I see his eyes shift, I swipe up on the ball. It bounces off his chin and into my hands. I whip it to Lucas on the right wing; Colin hustles over to guard him. Lucas puts his shoulder down and drives to the hoop, Colin with him stride for stride. Lucas goes up, powers through the contact, and scores.

We'd done it!

As I rush to high-five Lucas, Colin's voice rings out. "Foul. That was a charge."

"What?" I howl.

"You heard me. That was a charge. No basket. Our ball."

"Oh, come on," I say. "If anything, you fouled him."

Instead of answering, Colin picks up the basketball and inbounds to Bo, who catches it right by the hoop and lays it in.

"Game," Bo says. "We win."

"You're going to count that?" I bark in disbelief. "We weren't set."

"That's your fault for arguing."

I'm trembling with rage. "This is so—"

I don't finish. From the side of the court comes a wailing sound. Megan has her head in her hands and her shoulders are hunched. Lucas rushes to her and leads her back to their house.

"What's wrong with her anyway?" Colin asks, a snicker in his voice.

"Nothing's wrong with her," I answer.

He tilts his head and gives me a half smile. "If you say so." Then he turns to Bo. "Let's get out of here."

Around eight that night I notice a pickup truck parked in front of Lucas's house. I watch as Richard loads a few boxes, rides his motorcycle up a ramp, secures it, shakes Bill's hand, shakes Lucas's hand, hugs Megan, and drives away.

36

THE NEXT DAY IS THE last swimming session. There is no organized lesson that day—just free swim. After about ten minutes, somebody suggests playing Marco Polo. We're in high school, and it's a kid's game, but why not? "You want to be partners?" Hanna asks, and then she splashes water in my face.

"Sure," I say, though I don't understand how you have a partner in Marco Polo. Then I get it. If she takes off for one corner, I follow. And if I take off, she's right behind me.

Pretty soon, Marco Polo turns boring, and the kids stop. The sun comes out from behind the clouds. Hanna pops out of the pool, quickly wraps herself in a towel, and sits on the edge of the pool, dangling her legs in the water. I climb out and sit next to her. We talk about school, how we do and don't want summer to end. I feel somebody's foot on my back and turn. It's Colin, with Bo behind him.

"We're going to dive from the high board."

I shrug. "Go ahead."

"No, I mean we're *all* going to do it. It'll be our goodbye," he says.

Hanna stands to join them.

"I'll watch from here," I say.

"Afraid?" Bo says.

"I'm not afraid."

"Well, come on, then," Colin says.

I've never liked heights. The ladder goes up and up, making me dizzy. When I still have eight rungs to go, Colin has reached the top. He strides out to the edge, bounces a few times, and dives. I watch him fall and fall and finally split the water. There's a small splash, and then long seconds pass before he comes up, grinning. Next Bo dives. His body isn't as straight, and he makes a bigger splash. When he surfaces, he lets out a howl. Now Hanna is on the board, and I'm at the top rung, my heart pounding. I don't see her dive because the whole world has gone blurry. I do hear the cries from below.

"Let's go, Dravus! Your turn! What are you waiting for!"

I step onto the board. Far, far below, Bo and Colin and Hanna are treading water as they look up at me. I inch out, feel the give of the board, my head reeling.

I want to jump feetfirst, but know that would be wussy. "You going to dive or not!" I hear Bo scream, laughter in his voice, and I wonder how long I've been standing at the edge.

I picture the Olympic divers, take a deep breath, and fling myself out. I feel okay—even great—for a moment. But then I sense that my body is angled, and I have no clue how to straighten myself. Next thing, my face smacks the water, followed by my chest and stomach.

I'm under, water churning around me, but which way is up? I see light, swim to it. As my head rises above the surface, I spot Colin and Bo, their arms resting in the gutter that runs along the edge of the pool, laughing. Hanna is with them, but she isn't laughing.

I swim to them.

"I've seen belly flops before," Colin says, "but that's the first face flop I've ever seen."

Hanna puts her hand on my shoulder. "You okay?"

I nod, unsure if my voice works.

"Really?"

I swallow. "I'm fine. I just need to sit for a while."

The rest of the afternoon is vague. How long did I sit there? I don't know. Did Hanna sit with me? I don't know. I remember Bo or Colin telling me that they wouldn't be stopping by my house for hoops, and I remember saying that was fine. I don't remember riding my bike home.

Lucas? Megan? Are they in front of their house waiting for me? No idea. I'm pretty sure I eat some lunch, and for sure I go up to my room. I open my window and lie down on my bed, thinking fresh air and rest will help.

Next thing, I hear my mom's voice. "Nate, are you in there?"

I sit up just as she opens my door a crack to peer in.

"Were you sleeping?" she asks, totally perplexed.

If I tell her about my dive, it'll be straight to Dr. Charles to check for a concussion—with the risk of months away from basketball.

"I don't feel good," I say. "My stomach."

"Did they have food at the pool?"

"Yeah," I lie. "Last-day party. Probably something there got me."

"Have you been throwing up?"

"No. Just a gut ache. I'll be okay."

"All right. I'll leave you, then. But take it easy, and I'll make you chicken noodle soup for dinner. How's that sound?"

I force myself to go down for dinner and eat the soup. "That should soothe your stomach," my mom says before I return to my room.

I plop down on my bed, a black cloud over me. This can't be another concussion. Tryouts are a few months away; I need to play basketball every spare minute to have a chance to make the JV team.

Another knock on my door.

When I open it, my dad, smiling, hands me a couple of tablets of Pepto Bismol. "If you're fighting the Big D," he says, "these will help."

He stands, waiting, so I tear the plastic wrap off two pink tablets and chew them down.

"I'll leave the box with you," he says. "You can take four more tonight if you need to, but no more than four. The only thing worse than diarrhea is constipation."

37

WHEN I AWAKEN THE NEXT day, I lie still, waiting for the headache. Nothing. I brush my teeth, comb my hair. Still nothing. When I head downstairs, though, a throbbing begins. It's not horrible, it's just there, like the sound of a bass from somebody's car radio parked a block away.

Saturday is chore day: sweep the garage, mow the lawn, wash the car. The throbbing stays at a low level. Since my parents think I'm fighting diarrhea, I have toast and applesauce and a banana for lunch, which is okay. When I finish eating, I go outside. I look across the street—Lucas and Megan are out front.

"Hey," I say. "You want to shoot some?"

I think I might be able to take him on in a game, but once the ball bounces a couple of times and the throbbing rises a notch, I knew that's not happening. "I'm not feeling great," I say. "Maybe just HORSE."

I want to stay outside, but the throbbing increases by the minute. I go in, and Mom looks surprised. "Stomach still?"

"Just a little," I say.

"Lie down and rest, and drink water. If you're not feeling better by Monday, we'll go see Dr. Charles."

I nod, but I can't see Dr. Charles. It's too risky.

Sunday, I tell my parents that I'm going to Golden Gardens beach with some kids from school. "Would some of those kids be girl kids?" my dad teases. "That Hanna, for example?"

"No," I say too quickly.

Mom looks at me. "No?"

"Well, maybe she'll be there, but—" I stop, too confused to string my words together.

They both grin. "Have a good time," my dad says.

I ride my bike to Golden Gardens and lock it up. It's a hot day for Seattle. Volleyball nets are set up on the beach. On the grassy field east of the beach, people are throwing Frisbees, kicking soccer balls around, playing Wiffle ball. A line of about twenty people stretches out from the window where you can buy ice-cream cones and hot dogs. I see an eagle in one of the trees; sailboats, kayaks, and windsurfers are out on Puget Sound.

I sit on the beach, hating Colin and Bo for making me dive and hating myself for diving. When the sun gets too hot, I climb the crumbling staircase to upper Golden Gardens and find a bench in the shade of huge evergreens, where I watch dogs in the off-leash area chase one another.

It's all normal dog stuff until a Chihuahua goes after a

German shepherd. Then there's deep growling and high-pitched yelping. The Chihuahua owner pulls her dog away, but he keeps yapping and the shepherd keeps barking. Finally, the dogs are separated and are back on leashes. That's when I realize that no sound has reverberated inside my skill. No throbbing, no headache, no nothing.

38

THE NEXT AFTERNOON, LUCAS COMES over with Megan. First thing, I level with him about my dive—if you could call it that—and the headache. "I'm feeling better, but shooting around might be all I'm good for," I say.

"Fine by me," he says.

Megan makes more shots than ever and gets high fives from Lucas. Once, I take a step toward her, thinking I might high-five her, but her eyes go scared and I step back.

Just before I call it quits, I challenge Lucas to a one-on-one game, wanting to find out how far I am from normal. I don't push myself, going maybe seventy-five percent. Lucas dials his game back to give me a chance—the first time he's ever gone less than one hundred percent.

The score is tied 10–10 when he does a jab step to clear space for a jump shot. Instead of going up, he stumbles and goes down. Half of the sole of his shoe comes off, throwing him off-balance.

We both stare at the shoe for a moment, and then our eyes catch. "I got to go," he says, getting up.

He takes Megan by the hand, and they cross the street to his house, his shoe flapping with every step.

That night at dinner I ask my dad if I can get new shoes for school. He looks down at my feet. "You've got some wear left in those. How about we get you a pair just before tryouts. That's what? November? I was thinking something special, too. Maybe a LeBron James signature model."

I take a deep breath and then explain what happened to Lucas's shoes. "I thought if I got new ones, I could give him my old ones."

Mom screws up her face. "Putting on somebody's old shoes."

The table goes quiet, and then my dad speaks. "Big 5 always has good sales. We'll go after dinner and get two pairs. Tell him it was a two-for-one sale, so he won't feel like he owes you anything."

"You're okay with Big 5 instead of LeBron James?" Mom asks.

"Big 5 is fine," I say.

We go as soon as I get the dishwasher going. We find some Under Armour shoes that are okay. "Lucas is probably the same size as you," my dad says, "but we'll go up a half size to be safe. He can always wear two pairs of socks."

When we get back to the house, Lucas and Megan are across the street, shooting at their hoop. He's wearing the same shoes as before, only now he has duct tape holding the sole on.

I get out of the car and walk over to him, the box of shoes for him in my hand.

"Hey."

"Hey."

"My dad and I just went to Big 5. They had some shoes on sale. Two-for-one, so we ended up with an extra pair." I pause. "You can have these if you want. I'll outgrow them before I wear out my pair."

I'm thinking he won't take them, but he sits on the curb, takes his old shoes off, and pulls the new ones on.

They look big. "They fit?" I ask.

"Yeah. They're good."

"Okay."

I stay a moment longer, maybe waiting for him to say thanks, but he doesn't.

"Nate," my dad calls. "Time to get inside."

I get my shoes out of the car, go upstairs, and look out the window. He's running in place, then jumping, then moving side to side, getting the feel for his shoes.

39

EVERY DAY OVER LABOR DAY weekend the temperature reaches ninety. I get out early in the morning for my games against Lucas. In the afternoon we meet up again, but just to shoot around, play HORSE or Around the World, with Megan always getting her turn.

School starts the Wednesday after Labor Day. On Tuesday— the hottest day yet—my mom comes home early from work. She sees the three of us taking turns drinking water from the garden hose. "If you want, I could take you to Pop Mounger Pool," she says.

There aren't many outdoor pools in Seattle, and Pop Mounger in Magnolia is the best. Cool water on a hot day. I turn to Lucas. "What do you say?"

Before I finish the question, he's got Megan by the hand and has turned toward their house. "You go," he says, as if I'd asked him if he wanted to crawl through a sewer. Seconds later, he's disappeared into his shed.

I look at my mom.

"He might not know how to swim," she says softly.

"That can't be it," I say. "He's a really good athlete."

"Think about it, Nate," she says. "Where would he have learned? Who would have taught him? It's not something you just know how to do, even if you are an athlete." There's a long pause. "Do you want to go alone?"

I shake my head. "That's okay," I say.

40

THE NEXT MORNING, I SCARF down my bowl of Cheerios and eat my two pieces of toast, say goodbye to my parents, who are rushing to get themselves to work, and step out of the house. Lucas is standing in front of his house, Megan by his side. Up the block I spot her bus, two minutes away.

For a full year I'd avoided walking to Shilshole High with Lucas, so it feels natural to head off alone. After taking ten steps, though, I stop. All spring and summer we'd pushed each other hard on the basketball court, made each other better players.

I wait as the bus pulls up and the door hisses open. Lucas talks to the bus driver for a moment, sees Megan on, and they match hands against the glass until the bus drives off. He's surprised I've waited for him, but I bluff it, acting like it's something I always do. "Let me see your schedule," I say as we start down Seventeenth NW toward Shilshole High. "Maybe you've got some of the teachers I had last year."

He hands me a sheet of paper, and I glance at it. "You're in the honors program?"

He shrugs. "I get school."

"Those are all different teachers," I say, handing the schedule back.

His locker is in the A wing, mine is in the B wing, so we separate once we're inside the building. The first-day roar fills the halls. Back when I was a skinny freshman, I was terrified of that roar. Not anymore. I'm taller, have more muscle, and would have grown a wispy beard if I weren't afraid Amelia or my mom or my dad—or all of them—would razz me.

I have friends in every class. A wave here, a fist bump there. I sit next to Hanna in history, and Nicholas Putnam from rec basketball is my partner in art class. At lunch, I spot guys from the soccer team and find a chair at a table with them. I'm eating, listening to the talk about teachers and girls and how awful it is to be back at school, when I see Lucas across the room. "Hey, Cawley," I call out, "over here."

The guys I'm sitting with are startled. "Creepy Crawley?" one whispers. "You want him over here? The guy always looks like he wants to put his fist in your face."

I snort. "Yeah, well maybe if you got called *Creepy Crawley*, you'd want to smash someone, too. He's okay."

When Lucas sits down, the talk around us stops, but just for a few seconds. Then it resumes, loud and fast. Lucas doesn't say anything, but as time passes, he relaxes a little. He doesn't fit great with the other guys, but as a guy who quit soccer, I don't fit that well, either.

My first class after lunch is computer coding with Mr. Samanya, a laid-back guy from Thailand who likes to be called Mr. Sam. He's wearing a T-shirt with a picture of a guy at a desk looking at his computer. It reads I KEEP HITTING ESC, BUT I'M STILL HERE. He says hello to every student as they come in. I'd been nervous about the class ever since I'd seen it on my schedule, but he tells us to relax. "You're naturals," he says. "Just don't expect to come up with a million-dollar video game in one semester."

The last class of the day is PE, which has sixty kids divided into ten squads taught by two teachers. My teacher is Mr. Rodriguez, the JV basketball coach. The first thirty minutes are dedicated to stretching, running, and strength work, but the last twenty minutes are free time—basketball time for me. Mr. Rodriguez joins our game. He's not tall or fast, but he can flat-out shoot.

Walking home, I think about my day. All in all, it had been decent. My teachers and classes mostly look okay; still, something doesn't feel quite right. I almost reach my house before I realize what it was.

Amelia.

I thought Shilshole High would be better without her. I wouldn't be Amelia Dravus's not-as-smart, not-as-athletic little brother, but I miss her.

41

SO HERE'S MY ROUTINE. I go to class; I shoot hoops with Lucas after school; I do my homework. Most nights, after I switch off the light, I hear a basketball bouncing in the street, and I know it's Lucas, shooting in the dark at his sucky hoop. I want to join him, but that's such a no-go with my parents, I don't bother to ask.

A couple of times a week Amelia calls while I'm doing my homework. Mainly she talks to Mom, whose voice is low and muted. Then Dad gets on, and his cheery voice carries upstairs to my room. When he's done, he climbs the stairs and hands me the phone. I ask Amelia about Berkeley and soccer, she says things are going great, but I can tell she's faking it.

One night, after I hang up, I ask Mom what's wrong. "Cal is a big school with tough classes," she says, "and your sister hasn't yet found her stride with her team. She's got the stuff, though; she'll be fine. It'll just take some time."

In October I turn in my medical forms. I'm afraid Lucas

won't get his filled out, but he gets his completed at a community health clinic on Northwest Fifty-Sixth.

"Wouldn't it be something," I say to Lucas a week before tryouts, "if we end up as starters and Colin and Bo are stuck on the bench."

I'm half joking, but his eyes spark.

"We could do it," he says.

"In our dreams," I say.

"Why not?" he says. "We beat them that time, no matter what they say. We beat them. Right here on this court. You and me. We did it once, we can do it again. We just have to keep pushing each other, getting better every day. No quitting."

We're both quiet for a long time, and then I say, "I'm in."

"Me, too," he says.

We clasp hands, shoulder-high, sealing the deal.

42

IT'S A FRIDAY. BASKETBALL TRYOUTS are the next Monday. When I get home, Lucas is waiting for Megan's bus, which is no big deal since it's late at least twice a week.

I go inside, wolf down peanut butter with crackers, pull some shorts on, and grab my basketball. Three more days to prep. When I step outside, Lucas is standing in front of his house, still waiting. That isn't normal.

I cross the street.

"Her bus hasn't come yet?"

He shakes his head. "It's never been this late."

He doesn't own a cell phone, so I take out mine and offer it to him. "Call her school."

He stares at my iPhone like it's a grenade. It takes a second, but then I get it. How would he know how to use it?

I pull the phone back. "I'll call. She goes to Echohawk, right?"

"Yeah."

I wake up Siri. "Call Echohawk School in Seattle," I say.

"Calling Echohawk School," Siri replies.

I hear a ring, a woman's voice says "Echohawk School," and I hand Lucas the phone. He takes it and walks toward his house. As he talks, I fire up shots at his hoop. After a few minutes he turns back toward me and hands me my phone.

"What did they say?" I ask.

Lucas shakes his head. "They're calling 911."

From the shed, we hear the back-and-forth, back-and-forth of a board being sawed. "I need to tell Bill," Lucas says. "And my mom."

As he heads toward the shed, crows caw angrily in a nearby tree. A leaf blower goes on up the block. I stand there as the minutes pass, not sure what to do, until I see a police car driving fast down Seventeenth.

The car whips around the corner and pulls to a stop under the willow tree. The doors fly open, and a tall Black woman gets out from the driver's side; her partner, a balding old guy wearing thick glasses, emerges from the passenger's side.

I catch the woman's eyes, motion with my head toward Bill and Lucas, who have come out of the shed. As she walks to them, I cross the street and go into my house.

43

IT'S HALF AN HOUR LATER when my mother comes in. I hustle downstairs as soon as I hear her key in the door.

"Do you know what the police car is about?" she asks.

"It's Megan."

"Megan? What about Megan."

"She didn't come home on the bus," I say.

My mother's face turns gray. "You sure about this, Nate?"

"I was there when Lucas found out."

My mom pulls out her phone and looks at the screen. "No Amber Alert."

I follow her to a window, and we both stare out. As we watch, a second police car pulls up, and a wave of relief rolls over me. I'm certain Megan will step out.

But she doesn't.

"I'm going to call your father," Mom says, and she takes her phone into the kitchen. From the window I see Mr. Roth and

Mrs. Fiorini in the street, looking toward the Cawley house and talking.

Another half hour passes before Dad comes home. "She's probably somewhere in the school," he says as soon as he comes in the door. "They'll find her."

"I hope you're right," Mom says. "Her poor parents. I can't imagine what they're going through."

A mobile TV van pulls up in front of Lucas's house. "Does that say KOMO?" Mom asks.

"Yeah," I answer.

Dad turns on the TV, and we all watch. The KOMO weather report comes on, followed by a commercial for potato chips. "Come on, come on," Dad says. Then a woman's face fills the screen.

"This just in: Seattle student missing."

Megan's face fills the TV screen. I take in only snippets of what the woman is saying. "Special needs . . . Echohawk School . . . developing story . . ." And then Megan's face is replaced by a sports reporter talking about Sunday's Seahawks–Rams game.

My dad turns off the TV.

"I should get dinner going," Mom says.

"I'll help," Dad says. Then he turns to me. "It'll be okay, Nate. You'll see."

I go upstairs and drop onto my bed, my mind racing. What if some predator has her? No one says it, but that's what everyone is thinking. I picture Megan. Her scared eyes. She's been around me for months, yet when I smile at her or say "Good shot," she turns away, fearful. I've stopped trying to give her a high five. You hear the word *evil*, and it's just a word, but if some sicko has taken her, then this is the real thing.

My mom calls up to me, and I go downstairs and eat something for dinner, but I don't taste it. When we finish, my dad puts his hands on the table. "I'm going to call Pagliacci, order a couple of pizzas for the Cawleys. Nate, when we get them, you can bring them over."

Dad orders the pizzas, and while we wait, he turns on the TV and surfs news channels. Nothing. Mom logs into the Seattle Police Department's X feed. Megan's picture is posted, but there is no news. It's the same thing on the Nextdoor app.

The pizzas arrive, and I bring them over. When I near the walkway, a cop stops me. I explain, give the pizzas to him. "I'll make sure they get them," he says.

44

AFTER WE EAT, MOM AND Dad talk about whether they should call Amelia. I listen for a while, then go upstairs and lie on my bed. My mind keeps going back to my health classes and how the teacher said that when a kid goes missing, the first five hours are the most important.

After a while, I go to my window and look out toward the Cawleys'. It's windy, and the shadows from the branches of the corkscrew willow glide up and down the street with each new gust. What I want is for Lucas to come out and shoot hoops. That would mean everything is okay, but he doesn't.

Around ten I shower, turn off the light, and get in bed. I'm sure I won't sleep. I see midnight, then one a.m. and two a.m., but I don't see three. When I wake up on Saturday morning, I hear my parents talking in the kitchen and head downstairs. Mom is on her iPad; Dad is at the window looking over at Lucas's house.

"Anything?" I ask.

Dad pushes the *Seattle Times* toward me. Megan's picture is on the front page. "The police are asking businesses and residents to check their security cameras," he says. "Something will break."

I feel sick as I read the article. The writer describes Megan as intellectually disabled. He says that she suffers from anxiety, that she's mostly nonverbal, that she's extremely vulnerable. It's horrible that all those personal things are being made public, but even more horrible that she's still missing.

The day drags on. After I eat some lunch, Mom tells me to go somewhere and do something. "Bring your phone," she says, "I'll call if there's anything new."

I walk down to the Ballard Locks, cross the footbridge into Magnolia, then climb Commodore Way until I reach Discovery Park. On the open field by the water tower, people are throwing balls to their dogs, playing Frisbee. It's just a regular day. I take the wooded trail down to the lighthouse, sit on a boulder, and look out at Puget Sound. When the wind comes up and I smell rain in the air, I head home.

For dinner, Dad orders Pagliacci pizza again, this time for us and for the Cawleys. As we eat, Mom checks the police X account and Nextdoor on her iPad. "Somebody had to have seen her," she says, frustration in her voice.

45

ON SUNDAY MORNING THE CAWLEYS' house looks deserted, even though there's still a police car out front. As I eat breakfast, my dad has the TV on with the sound muted, and my mom stares out the window.

"Something's happening," my mom says as I'm finishing my toast. Dad and I rush to the window. A second police car has pulled up; both doors are open, and two cops are hurrying to the Cawleys' front door.

Before they reach it, Bill, Lucas, Lucas's mother, and Richard are out of the house. Bill and Lucas's mom get in the back seat of one police car; Lucas and Richard get in the other. The doors close, and both cars speed off.

My dad grabs the remote to the TV and cranks up the volume. There's some news program on, and they're talking about Ukraine. Dad switches channels, then switches back. More talk about Ukraine, then a commercial. Just as he's about to switch channels again, the words *BREAKING NEWS* are splashed on the screen. "This just in," the reporter says. "Megan Cawley, the special needs student who has been missing since Friday, has been found. Preliminary reports from the police department indicate that she is unharmed and in good health. Right now, she is being transported to Harborview Hospital, where she will meet her family and stay overnight for observation. To repeat, missing Seattle student Megan Cawley has been found unharmed."

Mom drops onto the sofa, puts her head in her hands, and sobs. Dad sits next to her and hugs her. "It's okay," he says, his voice shaky. "It's over." My throat is so tight I can hardly breathe.

"I have to call Amelia," Mom says finally. "She needs to know."

What happened comes out over the next few hours. A substitute bus driver dropped Megan off in front of a house on North Seventy-Seventh, instead of Northwest Seventy-Seventh. She wandered around a while before she found an unlocked shed behind a house on Dayton, which is where she stayed for the next forty hours, drinking bottled water and eating peanut butter from an earthquake emergency kit the homeowner kept out there. On Sunday morning, the owner went to get some gardening tools, found her, and called 911.

46

MEGAN IS SAFE, AND I know that's the most important thing, but that night I can't stop thinking about basketball tryouts. Lucas and I had pushed each other hard, and we were ready. But would he even be there? Every time I wake up during the night, I go to my window, hoping to see a light in his house.

Nothing.

In the morning his house still looks and feels empty. I wait as long as I can, hoping his door will open and he'll come out, but eventually I give up and walk to Shilshole alone. In the halls, kids I hardly know come up and ask me questions. "I don't know anything more than what was on TV," I answer over and over.

All day I keep looking for him in the hallways. Megan is okay—that's what they said on the news. Tired and scared, but okay. If doctors kept her overnight in the hospital, that meant she'd return home in the morning. Lucas could make it to school in time for the tryouts.

So why isn't he here?

During warm-ups, I fire up a few shots, short-arming everything, still hoping Lucas will walk through the gym door, ready to go. The whistle blows, and all of us—I count over thirty—form a half circle around Mr. Varner, the varsity coach. Mr. Smiley, the assistant coach, and Mr. Rodriguez, the JV coach, stand off to the side. I take deep breaths to slow my breathing and calm myself. It doesn't work. Lucas was going to have my back, and I was going to have his. That was the plan. Instead, I'm on my own.

Coach Varner starts us out with simple drills. Chest passes. Bounce passes. Lay-ins. I'm terrible at everything, as if my muscles are mush. After that, he has each of us shoot a midrange jumper from the wing, a three-pointer from the top of the key, and a free throw, as Smiley and Rodriguez record the results. I miss all my shots. When the scrimmages start a few minutes later, I double dribble twice in the first few minutes. I play a little better after that, making a steal and grabbing a couple of rebounds, and then it's over.

I walk home, but before I go inside my house, I look at Lucas's house. Their porch light is on. Had it been on in the morning? I can't remember.

When I step inside my front door, my mom is waiting for me.

"How'd tryouts go?" she says.

"I sucked," I answer, then motion with my head toward the Cawleys' house. "Are they back?"

She nods. "A van brought them twenty minutes ago. Some sort of hospital transportation, I guess. Anyway, they're all home."

"That's great," I say. "Megan must be okay."

"Maybe physically," Mom says, "but getting over this emotionally will take her a long time."

"Do you think—" I say, and I stop.

"Do I think what?" she asks.

"Do you think Lucas will go to school tomorrow?"

"Is this about tryouts?"

"No," I say. "Well, yeah."

She tilts her head and sighs. "Nate, I know you worked out together, but all you can do now is focus on what you can control and let everything else go."

47

WHEN I STEP OUTSIDE THE next morning, Lucas is waiting for me. For a split second I think he's going to school, and a spark fires through me, but only for a second. He doesn't have his backpack; he's not wearing a jacket. Something's not right.

"Good to see you," I say, trying to sound normal. "I'm so—"

"Yeah, yeah," he says, cutting me off. "Look, I'm going into Echohawk with Megan. They think she'll do better if I'm with her in class and on the bus. You know, help her readjust."

"That makes sense," I say.

He nods. "They called the principal at Shilshole High to clear it with her. She's going to have the teachers send my assignments to Mrs. Spahn in the office. I said that you'd pick them up for me. Is that okay?"

"Sure," I say. "No worries."

He turns and points to a cardboard box by his back door. "Just put whatever she gives you in there."

"How long will you go in with Megan?" I ask.

"A week," he says. "After that, they say she needs to go on her own."

Neither of us says anything about tryouts, because there's nothing to say.

Since I know how things stand, I'm not looking for Lucas in the hallways, which makes the day easier. I follow along in my classes, laugh at dumb jokes at lunch, make progress on my programming project for Mr. Sam. After the final bell, I hustle to the office to get Lucas's packet of work. As soon as I see the line of kids waiting to talk with Mrs. Spahn, my stomach turns over. After my first miserable day at tryouts, I can't be late for day two.

I catch a break. Mrs. Spahn spots me, stops what she is doing, picks up a large manila envelope, and brings it to me. "Tell Lucas we're all thinking about him and his sister," she says.

I tell her I will and hustle out of there.

In the gym, after we've warmed up, Coach Rodriguez calls out a bunch of names, including mine. We're the first cut. "Come with me," he says, and he leads us to the east court, where we'll compete for spots on the junior varsity.

Away from the varsity players, I play better in the scrimmage—making solid passes, covering my guy on defense, even nailing a couple of shots.

I'm on the Black team, and we trail the Reds by one, with time running out. As I bring the ball into front court, Coach Rodriguez calls out, "Last possession." Wally Harter is guarding me, but as I near the top of the key, Dustin Long leaves his man to double-team. Our center, Tony Nevin, is open at the free throw, waving for the ball. A simple pass from me would give him a good look at the game winner. Instead, I go into hero-ball mode, rising for a contested jump shot that misses long. When a guy on the Red team grabs the rebound, Coach Rodriguez blows his whistle. "That's it. See you all tomorrow."

Nevin glares at me as he walks off the court. I wait, letting him get clear before I head out. I take a couple of steps when Rodriguez's voice stops me. "Dravus," he calls out, and I turn to face him. "This is a team game," he says. "You get what I'm saying?"

I nod and drag myself off the court.

48

WEDNESDAY—LAST DAY OF TRYOUTS. I shoot better in warm-ups, run the fast break drill better, feel more relaxed. When the scrimmage starts, Coach Rodriguez matches me up against Patrick Colligan, a guy who'd played for the North Beach Sharks in rec league.

I'd handled Colligan in those games, so I should have handled him at tryouts, and I could have—only I'm so afraid of taking another selfish shot that I pass up open looks, forcing the ball to teammates who aren't open. A couple of turnovers lead to breakaway buckets for Colligan, and then I foul him trying to make a steal, and halfway through the scrimmage I'm totally out of sync, and I stay that way to the end.

After the final whistle Coach Rodriguez thanks us for trying out. "I'll post the roster outside the main office tomorrow morning. You guys that don't make it? Play intramurals or play in a rec league and then turn out again next year. Remember, Michael Jordan didn't make his school team the first time he tried out."

I'm sure I'm getting cut. As I'm heading toward the locker room, for the second straight day Coach Rodriguez tells me to stay a minute.

"The JV team usually has twelve players," he says, "but I'm going to keep you on as number thirteen. You didn't show much in tryouts, but Ethan Chan told me you were rock solid on his rec team, and your sister is a legend around here, so you've got good genes. Here's the thing, though. No guarantee that you'll play a single minute, and I don't want any phone calls from Mom or Dad if you don't. Understood?"

My parents are in the kitchen when I step through the front door.

"So?" Dad asks. "How'd it go?"

"I sort of made the team," I answer.

His eyebrows go up. "How do you *sort of* make a team?" he asks, so I explain.

"Well, *sort of* is better than being cut," Mom says. "And even if you don't get any playing time, the practices will get you primed for rec league in the spring."

That night, Amelia calls. Before Mom ends the call, she brings her cell upstairs to me.

"Hey," Amelia says, "I hear you made JV."

"Only because Ethan Chan said good things."

She laughs. "He owed you. You were his go-between on the senior prom, right?"

"Yeah," I admit. "But I didn't know you knew."

"It took a while," she says, "but I figured it out. It's so Ethan. He always scopes out the situation before he does anything."

"I'd feel better if I made the JV team without his help," I say.

"You made the team, Nate. That's what counts. JV will be more fun than varsity. Less pressure. You just play for fun."

I'm about to tell her that I probably won't play at all, when I hear two quick beeps. "That's my coach," she says, and she disconnects.

49

THE VARSITY TEAMS PRACTICE AFTER school, which means JV
practices are six thirty in the morning. As I head off, it's so dark I
can see stars in the sky. During practice, it's hard to get my body
going, but it's hard for everybody. Even Coach Rodriguez is
yawning. "We'll get used to this," he says, and I hope he's right.

When I return home that afternoon, Lucas is shooting at his
hoop.

"You want to shoot over here?" I ask, motioning with my
head toward my basket.

"Here is okay," he answers.

That's when I spot Megan, standing in the shadow of the
shed.

I join Lucas on his hoop. We've been shooting a few minutes when Richard comes out, a backpack over his shoulders
and saddle bags in his hand. He straps the saddle bags onto the
back of his motorcycle and then walks over to us. "I'm off, little

bro," he says to Lucas, giving him a high handshake. "You're good here, right?"

Lucas nods, but his face and body say the opposite. Richard pretends not to notice and turns to Megan. "Hey, Sis, monster hug, okay?"

Megan gives him a big hug, holding on for a long time. Finally, Richard breaks free, pulls his helmet on, fires up the motorcycle, and rides off. After he disappears around the corner, Lucas turns to me. "You want to go one-on-one?"

We haven't played a real game since Megan's disappearance. Maybe I forgot how hard he plays and how quick he is. Maybe his anger comes out on the court. Whatever the reason, he annihilates me 11–4 and 11–2.

"We can stop," he says, wiping the sweat from his forehead after the second game.

"One more."

This time I go at him with the same fury he has when he comes at me, fighting for every rebound, contesting every jump shot, blocking every drive, playing the way I should have played during tryouts.

I'm up 10–9 with the ball. I fake a jump shot, drive toward the hoop for the winning lay-in. His hand swipes at the ball, trying for the block but catching me on the side of my head instead, making me lose my balance. I still get my shot up, but as the ball goes through the hoop, I hit concrete, tearing the skin off my right knee. "Good game," he says as he reaches down and pulls me to my feet.

Blood is streaming down my leg. "I should take care of this," I say, and I limp across the street toward my home.

"I was going for the ball," he calls after me.

"I know," I say, turning back.

My mom came home while we were playing. When she sees my knee, her face contorts. "In the kitchen and quick. I don't want blood on the carpet."

I sit on a chair as she dabs the wound with rubbing alcohol that hurts like crazy. "Rough game?"

"Just a fall."

"Stand," she says after she'd bandaged me up. I stand. "Feel okay?"

"Feels fine."

"Not too tight?"

"No. It's perfect. Thanks."

The front door opens, and my dad steps in. "Anybody home?" he says as he drops his keys into a wooden box he keeps by the door.

"In here," Mom calls.

"What happened?" Dad says when he sees the bandage around my knee.

"Just a scrape," I say.

"A little more than a scrape," Mom says. "He lost a chunk of flesh."

Dad snorts. "You know, there are these things called knee-pads. NBA guys used to wear them. I could get you some."

"I'm not wearing kneepads," I say, and head upstairs to my room.

✕ ✕ ✕

After that, every afternoon Lucas and I go one-on-one, always using his hoop so Megan can stay where she feels safe. Once the third game ends, Lucas has me show him what I'd done at JV practice, though nothing is new.

50

THE OPENING GAME OF THE season is at home on Friday afternoon against North Central High. It's a JV game that nobody cares about, but my heart starts racing anyway.

Patrick Colligan and Wally Harter are the starters at guard. Pedro Lima and Greg Domingo are backups. That leaves me as the fifth guard. I know I'm better than all of them, but it's fair. I play free and loose against Lucas, but at JV practice my legs are stuck in mud.

Before the game, Coach Rodriguez gives a pep talk on playing for the love of the game, not the score. I nod, but the best players are always looking for something to be mad about. To win, you need some attitude.

In the first quarter, behind tough man-to-man defense, we jump out to a ten-point lead. In the second, Coach Rodriguez switches to a zone to keep his starters from wearing out. By halftime North Central has tied the game.

We go back to the man-to-man in the third quarter, but

North Central is no longer intimidated—not after clawing back—and they hang tough.

Sitting on the bench, I keep seeing plays I could make, weaknesses I could exploit. The lead seesaws, neither team able to pull away. With twenty seconds left, we are up by one. As Colligan brings the ball across the center line, his defender comes out on him—too close. "Drive on him!" I scream from the bench. "Take him!"

Instead of slashing to the hole, Colligan picks up his dribble. The guy guarding him swats at the ball, stripping it loose. It bounds toward the sideline, where another North Central player retrieves it and is off. His lay-in kisses off the glass, drops through, the horn sounds, and North Central is celebrating.

My guts are in a knot, but Coach Rodriguez is clapping his hands. "Good effort! Be proud of yourselves!" he says as we huddle. "Now go shake their hands."

51

SOFT DEFENSE IN CRUNCH TIME—THAT'S why we lose the second and third games of the season. By the fourth game—another loss—we are playing soft defense all the time, and once that happens, the losses keep coming. Five, six, seven, eight. I'm playing better at practice, so I'm getting a few minutes in games, but not many.

Coach Rodriguez stays upbeat, talking about playing for the love of the game and not worrying about the score. Pedro Lima and a backup forward, Chuck Simpson, start mocking him, calling him Hakuna Matata and humming the song when he gives his pep talks.

Coach Rodriguez isn't entirely clueless. A couple of times he snaps, "What's the joke?" when he catches guys smiling. Nobody says anything, but Lima and Simpson keep humming the song, and other guys snicker.

After the eighth loss, Lima and Simpson skip practice.

Coach Rodriguez sits them in our next game against Nathan Hale High, giving me Lima's normal minutes. I'm playing alongside Greg Domingo on the second team, but we can't get in sync. When I'm expecting him to go backdoor, he pops out for a pass. When I think he wants to switch on defense, he stays with his man. Once, I hit him in the face with a pass he isn't expecting.

All through the game Lima and Simpson sit at the end of the bench, elbowing one another, humming, and making jokes. Nathan Hale is leading by twenty-two halfway through the fourth quarter when Coach Rodriguez calls a time-out. As the team huddles, he points to Lima and Simpson. "You two check in for Domingo and Dravus."

They exchange a look and drag themselves, shoulders slumped, toward the scorer's table. Coach Rodriguez notices and calls them back. "If you don't want to play, just tell me. Other guys will take your minutes."

Lima shrugs. "Whatever."

Coach Rodriguez's eyes narrow. "No. Not *whatever*. Yes or no."

Lima opens his hands. "Whatever," he repeats.

Coach Rodriguez looks to Simpson. "And you?"

A shoulder shrug and then, "Not feeling it today, Coach."

"Fine. Sit down, both of you." Domingo and I finish the game, leading the team on a 10–4 run in the final minutes.

As guys are changing into street clothes after the game, Coach Rodriguez's voice fills the space. "Lima, Simpson. Leave your uniforms on the bench. You won't be needing them."

Lima faces him. "You kicking us off the team?" he says.

"No," Coach Rodriguez replies. "You kicked yourselves off the team."

"That's clever," Simpson says, peeling off his jersey and flinging it down. "Ha! Ha! Only you're the joke. Every player on this team is laughing at you. Hakuna Matata. That's what we call you."

Coach Rodriguez's voice is a menacing growl. "Go on. Get out of here."

52

IT'S CHRISTMAS, AND THE WHOLE family gets lucky. The Missoula grandparents are on a cruise in the Caribbean. Amelia comes home. She spends ninety percent of her time with her friends, but having her around makes the house feel more normal. There's no practice, so Lucas and I go at it in the morning and then again in the afternoon, no matter the weather.

On Amelia's last night before returning to Berkeley, she surprises me by asking if I want to play miniature golf at Interbay. "Unless you can think of something else," she says.

It's cold, windy, and drizzling. The guy behind the counter looks at us as if we're crazy. "You sure you don't want to just hit a bucket?" he asks. "The stalls are covered and heated, and you can borrow clubs."

The drizzle turns into rain on the sixth hole, so our miniature golf turns into speed miniature golf. The weather is so miserable, it's fun. When we finish, we go to Larsen's and get hot chocolates and almond pastries. She asks about my team, and I tell her we haven't won a single game.

"How about you?" she asks. "You getting much playing time?"

"Not yet," I say, "but a couple of guys got kicked off, so I should get more."

Her eyebrows go up. "You know you got a mustache going there, Bro."

I think she's talking about the chocolate, so I wipe my mouth. "No," she says. "I mean a real mustache. You growing it out? The Freddie Mercury look?"

"Stop!" I say.

Her face turns serious. "Guys like Colin and Bo," she says, "they're good athletes and all. I'm not saying they aren't. But they got a head start on you. You know what I mean—with their bodies. Not everybody hits puberty at the same time. You're catching up now. What I'm saying is—don't give them too much credit. Just because they were better than you in grade school doesn't mean they'll always be better than you."

I want to answer, but my mouth has gone dry and I know my face is flushed. Amelia smiles. "I get the feeling you don't like talking about puberty with your sister."

"You got that right," I say, and my voice cracks on *right*. A pause, and we both laugh.

"How about Lucas?" she asks after a silence. "Is he on the team?"

I shake my head. "The thing with Megan happened just before tryouts, so he missed them."

"And the coach didn't give him a look later on?" she says.

I shake my head.

"He should have," she says. "What a jerk."

"That's not fair," I say. "How would Coach Rodriguez know that Lucas plays basketball?"

She looks at me, starts to say something, and then stops.

The next morning, when my parents drive her to the airport, I go along. When my mom pulls up at the Alaska Airlines door, Amelia hops out, hugs Mom and Dad, and then hugs me.

On the ride home, I sit in the back seat with my eyes closed, pretending to sleep. It's quiet for a while, and then I hear my mom. "That was quick," she says. "Her classes don't start for another week."

"Probably a boyfriend," Dad says.

Mom scoffs. "Yeah. Well, she's got months to be with him. It wouldn't have hurt her to spend more of the break with her parents."

"She's nineteen," Dad says.

"So, you don't mind?" Mom says, an edge to her voice.

"No, I mind. I'm just trying—"

"Trying to what?" Mom interrupts.

"Trying to get used to being unimportant."

53

AMELIA HADN'T SAID IT, BUT I know what she was thinking. I should have stepped up for Lucas. I still could, especially now that Simpson and Lima are off the team. Before I talk to Rodriguez, though, I need to talk to Lucas.

The next morning, I cross the street and peek inside the shed. Immediately I'm hit with a heavy chemical smell. Lucas and Bill are spraying a sealant on about a dozen finished flower boxes. Megan slides them out of the way when they finish.

Bill spots me first. "Hello, Nate," he says.

"Hello, Bill," I answer.

Calling him that never feels right, but "Mr. Cawley" seems even more wrong. Lucas looks up, motions to the door, and I follow him out into the fresh air. "What's up?" he asks.

"I might be able to get you on the JV team," I say.

"How?"

"Two guys just got kicked off for being jerks," I say. "I can tell Coach Rodriguez that Ethan Chan picked you as MVP of our rec team. Rodriguez respects Coach C. Are you interested?"

His mind works for a while. "Yeah, I'm interested."

Early Monday morning, I tap on Coach Rodriguez's office door. He opens up, coffee cup in hand, and scowls at me. "You quitting, too."

"No," I say. "Not me. No. Never."

His face relaxes. "So what can I do for you?"

I explain about Lucas. As I speak, his eyes brighten, pleased to learn that someone wants to join his team. "Yeah, yeah. I remember there were two players Ethan Chan told me about, but his name didn't stick. It was his sister who went missing?"

I nod.

"I didn't make the connection," he says. "I should have, but I didn't. What happened was terrible."

"He's a warrior," I say. "There's no quit in him, and I know he turned in his paperwork."

Coach Rodriguez snorts. "Well, this team is nothing but *quit* right now. Bring him along."

The next morning, Lucas is tentative in the warm-ups and the drills, but once the scrimmage starts, he's Hurricane Lucas, crashing the boards, ball-hawking on defense, driving hard to the hole. The other guys have stunned looks on their faces.

I'm afraid Rodriguez will dial Lucas back, but instead it's "That's good. I like your toughness." The praise gets my juices flowing, too. Soon it isn't just Lucas creating chaos; it's both of us. After Lucas knocks Colligan to the ground with a hard foul, Colligan pops up and shoves Lucas hard. Lucas shoves him back even harder, and fists are about to fly before guys pull them apart.

During the final practices before the season resumes, everybody is intense. Rodriguez has Lucas and me as guards on the second unit, but we dominate Colligan and Harter in scrimmages, shutting them down defensively and taking it to them on offense. When practice ends, Coach Rodriguez sits all four of us down.

"Given our record," he says, his eyes scanning us, "we need to shake things up, so I'm going to start Dravus and Cawley. You two"—his eyes move to Colligan and Harter—"will come off the bench. I wanted you to know ahead of time. No surprises, and they'll be plenty of minutes to go around."

He leaves, and Colligan and Harter stare at us. Then Harter stands and sticks his fist out. "Just win, baby," he says, echoing the Raiders motto.

I bump his fist and then Lucas does, and then we bump fists with Colligan, and it's all good, or at least semi-good, though they both have to be chafing inside.

54

OUR FIRST GAME AFTER THE Christmas break is on the road against Shorewood High. They're 6–2 while we're 0–8, so they must figure they'll win easily.

Lucas and I start, and I'm hoping we're going to hit them hard early, but I'm so nervous that I turn the ball over a couple of times, and Lucas gets called for an over-the-back foul on a rebound. After three minutes, we're down six.

Rodriguez calls time, and I think he's going to yank us for Colligan and Harter. *Don't!* I'm screaming in my head, and maybe the vibes get through. He takes a deep breath. "It's a long game," he says.

We stay in.

We settle in, too. The other starters—Dustin Long, Tony Nevin, and Nicholas Putnam—aren't used to playing with us, so nothing is smooth. The fight is there, though, and that keeps the game close. Shorewood's eight-point lead never reaches ten, even with Colligan and Harter on the court while we're resting. A couple of times we close to within four, but we get no closer.

With just over one minute left in the fourth quarter, we have the ball, still down by six. I'd had three shots rim out in the second half, but when you're a shooter, you've got to keep shooting. The guy guarding me backs off, so I let it fly from behind the three-point line.

Perfect rotation . . . perfect arc . . . but an inch short. The ball hits the front rim, bounces up a foot or so, bounces on the front rim again, teeters, and then snuggles down and through the net. Shooter's roll.

Down three.

Their coach calls time-out to break our momentum; Coach Rodriguez has the answer. "Press," he says, his voice fiery. "Full court. All out. Let's win this thing!"

The press catches Shorewood by surprise. Lucas and I trap their point guard along the sideline. He panics, chucking a wild pass toward center court. Tony Nevin snags it and drives right down the lane for a layup.

Down one. Thirty-seven seconds on the clock.

Shorewood calls their last time-out to set up a play to beat our press. Coach Rodriguez does the smart thing and calls off the press. Because of the shot clock, they can't dribble out the game. If we get a stop, we'll have the final shot.

The Shorewood guards walk the ball up the court, letting seconds tick off the clock. Then everyone clears out, leaving their point guard to go one-on-one against me. He turns his back and slowly works his way into the lane, maneuvering toward his favorite spot on the court.

Before he reaches it, Lucas races over to double-team. The Shorewood guard twists his body between us, stumbles, and falls—holding the ball to his chest.

The whistle blows.

I stare at the ref, afraid he'll call a foul on me or Lucas. Instead, he bicycles his hands. "Traveling!"

I race to the sideline. The ref bounces the ball to me, and I inbound to Lucas, who drives toward the hoop. A Shorewood guy is set, waiting to take the charge. At the last second, Lucas pulls up. I'd been trailing the play, and he spots me. The ball is in my hands, and I'm up in my shooting motion before I have time to get nervous. I let it go, then watch, though I don't have to. This one doesn't need a lucky bounce.

It's just one win, but we're jumping around like we've taken the Metro title, and so is Coach Rodriguez.

55

AFTER THAT FIRST VICTORY, LUCAS'S confidence, or arrogance, or whatever you want to call it, infects the entire team. The guys at the end of the bench stalk onto the court with scowls on their faces and chips on their shoulders. Coach Rodriguez, his shoulders back and his spine straight, starts wearing a deep purple tie with a dark blue shirt, making him look like a mafioso.

We destroy Nathan Hale at home. Ingraham High, the second-best team in the league, fights hard for three periods, but they wilt in the fourth under the relentless pressure of our clawing defense. Against Roosevelt, we score the first ten points and never look back. We throttle Forest Park so completely that the refs keep the clock running to get the fourth quarter over with and end the slaughter. The wins just keep coming.

Our last game is against Lakeshore at their gym. With a record of 16–1, they've clinched a spot in the North Division playoffs. In warm-ups, I can see they're loose, but in an unfocused way. It's a nothing game to them.

Coach Rodriguez calls us together before game-time. "Forget their record. Play your game, and we can beat these guys."

I believe him—we all do because we believe in ourselves. Still, I expect a battle to the final buzzer. Even when we get off to a good start, I think wounded pride will motivate them. It doesn't happen. We're quicker to the ball, tougher on defense, more disciplined on offense. Our lead just grows and grows, like when a dam gives way and more and more water pours through. Somebody walking in from the street would guess we're the 16–1 team headed to the playoffs, while they're the nobodies going nowhere. The final score is 61–39.

I find out later that Lakeshore beat our varsity in our gym on a last-second three-pointer, knocking Colin and Bo out of the Metro playoffs and ending Coach Varner's chance for his first Metro title. It's too bad for Varner, but I'm okay with not seeing Colin and Bo strutting around the campus.

56

I THINK THAT LAKESHORE IS our last game, but it isn't. The next day, during an end-of-the-season cake and ice-cream party in a conference room, Coach Rodriguez tells us about a proposed JV versus varsity game to benefit the Ballard Food Bank. The principal, Ms. Clyburn, has agreed to let kids skip their final class of the day if they bring a can of food. "You don't have to do this," Rodriguez says, "but it is for a good cause."

"I don't know," Colligan says. "We've got a good feeling about this season. We get crushed by those guys in front of the entire school and . . ."

Silence.

Tony Nevin turns to Lucas. "What do you think?"

"I say play," he answers.

And that ends the discussion. The vote is 12–0 in favor of playing, with even Colligan raising his hand.

The game is Friday. On Wednesday, the *Seattle Times* names

Colin second team all-city, while Bo gets honorable mention. Thursday night, I'm so nervous I have trouble eating.

Mom notices. "The game is just for fun and to collect food, right?"

"I know," I answer.

"But you don't want to get your butt kicked," Dad says.

I nod. "That's it."

I eat as much as I can manage, clear my dishes, and am headed to my room when Mom calls me back. "How are the Cawleys doing?"

"What do you mean?" I ask.

"I mean how do they seem? Better? Worse? Stuck?"

I shrug. "Megan doesn't talk to me, but I've seen her laugh with Lucas a few times."

Mom frowns. "And what about Lucas? How's he doing?"

"I guess he's okay. We play ball, and that's it."

"You don't ever talk about anything but hoops?"

"Not really," I say.

My dad speaks from the kitchen. "Honey, that's the way most males are programmed. The Y chromosome just doesn't have much to say."

Mom scowls. "Yeah? Maybe the Y chromosome should learn."

Friday—game day—at lunch I'm eating with Colligan, Long, Nevin, and pretty much all the guys on the team. That has happened slowly over the season.

Lucas is there, too, though he never says anything. For a while I didn't get it, but then I make myself hear the conversation the way he hears it. Xboxes and Hulu and vacations to Mexico and Hawaii—to him it's a foreign language.

Halfway through lunch, Colin, with Bo a couple feet behind him as usual, stops at our table and looks us over. "The team that eats together loses together," he jokes. "We are going to mop the floor with you guys. Four quarters of total domination. You know that, right?"

"You talk a good game," Nevin says.

Colin smiles. "We play a good game, too. You'll see."

He raps the table a couple of times before walking away. When he's out of earshot, Colligan motions with his head toward Colin. "He can be such a jerk."

57

FINAL PERIOD.

Game-time.

The food bank barrels are overflowing because the gym is packed. The varsity team has played before big crowds, but it's a new experience for us and for Coach Rodriguez, too. His face is sweaty, and every few seconds he's wiping his forehead with a towel. "Just freewheel it out there," he says in our huddle. "You never know what might happen."

Dustin Long motions with his head toward the court. "How come Smiley is a ref?" he asks. "He's their assistant coach. And that's Colin's father, isn't it? Is he the other ref? That's not right."

"Don't worry about the officiating," Rodriguez answers. "Just concentrate on your play. On three!"

We count down, give a loud cheer, and it's game on.

As I take the court, my eyes wander to the rows behind the bench that are set aside for adults, and then I do a double take. My parents hadn't said anything about coming, but my mom and dad are there, which is a big deal because they almost never take time off. My mom raises her hands above her head and shouts, "Go, JVs!" while my dad catches my eye and gives me a thumbs-up.

Coach Rodriguez told us to freewheel it, but in the opening minutes we're tight. My first shot is an airball from about fifteen feet. Next time down, Nevin misses a layup. Dustin Long gets the offensive rebound but fumbles the ball out-of-bounds. Two minutes in, Colin nails a three-pointer over me, and we're down 9–0.

"Let me guard Colin," Lucas says to Coach Rodriguez during a quick timeout, and he's not asking, he's telling.

I dribble up court and hit Putnam, who'd flashed open. He rises for a jumper from the wing. He isn't trying to bank it home, but his shot is a line drive that rockets off the backboard and through.

As we hustle back on defense, Lucas picks up Colin at half-court and clings to him like a leech. He always plays tough defense, but there's a fury in his eyes that makes this different. Colin started the whole Creepy Crawley thing, and this is Lucas's chance for payback, with the whole school watching.

Twice he deflects Colin's passes, leading to easy buckets for us on the other end. After he deflects a third pass, Colin has Bo bring the ball up court, which disrupts their offensive sets. By the end of the first quarter we've cut the lead to four.

In the second quarter, Lucas still has Colin on lockdown, so they start feeding their center, Arthur Jacobson, a six-six guy with superlong arms who moves in a slithery, eel-like way that's hard to defend. Nevin tries, but Jacobson gets easy looks. They're up 28–20 at the half, and it would have been worse if Jacobson hadn't missed a couple of gimmes.

This isn't a real game, so both teams stay on the court through halftime, which is short. For a minute or so, Rodriguez paces around before kneeling in the middle of us all. "Listen," he says. "They dump the ball into Jacobson, somebody double-team immediately. Swipe at the ball, disrupt. Make him pass it back out. Only not you, Lucas. You stay on Colin."

They're the varsity, right? And we're the guys who got cut from the varsity. So, with an eight-point lead heading into the second half, you'd think they'd be confident, but Colin has no bounce to his step, and I see fear in his eyes.

In the third quarter, he doesn't even try to score. Their offense is all Jacobson. We're lousy at double-teaming, so he keeps getting good shots. We stay in the game only because Lucas takes it at Colin on the offensive end of the court. No settling for jump shots; he puts his shoulder down and drives.

With twenty seconds left in the third quarter and their lead at five, Nevin finally makes a defensive play, slapping the ball out of Jacobson's hands. Lucas snares the loose ball; I take off; he hits me at midcourt with a crisp pass. Bo is back, in good defensive position, so I pull up and shoot in rhythm from the top of the key. Nothing but net, cutting their lead to two after three quarters.

During the break, Rodriguez's voice races like an Indy car. "All right! All right! All right! We're here, in the game, in the fourth quarter. They're thinking how humiliating it will be to lose, and teams that think don't *play*." He goes on, talking faster and faster, until the horn sounds.

Back on the court, I hear a cheer roll down from the stands. "JV! JV! JV!" The hair on my arms and neck stands up. The whole school is behind us. In the adults' section, my mother is clutching my father's arm, both sets of eyes glowing with excitement.

Here's the problem: you can be too pumped, and that's what we are. On the varsity's first possession, Lucas goes for a steal but instead clobbers Colin, picking up his fourth foul. Fifteen seconds later I get called for a blocking foul that turns into a three-point play. A minute into the final quarter, we're down by eight again.

Rodriguez is up. "Time out!

"Keep playing tight defense," he says to Lucas. "You foul out, you foul out." Then he turns to the rest of us. "Don't be afraid to win. Play your game, not theirs."

That's what we do. We don't force passes, don't commit stupid fouls, take our shots when we're open, play solid D.

It works.

We whittle the lead down to four, then to two. Jacobson hits a short hook; Lucas rattles in a jumper from inside the free throw line to match it. Then Dustin Long makes a steal that leads to a breakaway bucket.

The game is tied.

I look at the clock.

Fifteen seconds.

Everybody in the gym is up, cheering. "JV! JV! JV!"

Bo inbounds to Colin, who walks the ball up court, Lucas on him. Jacobson claps his hands twice, calling for the ball. Instead of passing, Colin takes off like a shot toward the hoop, Lucas blanketing him. Colin goes up, twists in the air, but Lucas's hand is on the ball, blocking the shot. They both go down in a heap; the whistle blows.

The gym falls silent . . . waiting.

After a long moment, Smiley makes a karate chop with his right hand on his left wrist, points at Lucas, and raises two fingers above his head. Lucas's eyes fill with rage. He stands, stares Smiley down, but turns and walks away without saying a word.

The kids in the stands have let loose with a torrent of boos that fill the gym. Colin, with two seconds on the clock, settles in at the free throw line. The booing grows louder as he eyes the hoop, dribbles twice, and drains his first free throw.

The numbers on the scoreboard change from 49–49 to 50–49.

Colin clanks the next free throw on purpose, leaving us no time to set up a play. Nevin grabs the rebound, spins, and heaves the ball toward our hoop. It falls twenty feet short as the horn sounds.

58

THE VARSITY GUYS HEAD OUT, but we linger in the hallway as kids give us fist bumps and tell us how great we played. One of them is Hanna. "You almost beat them," she says, smiling, which surprises me.

It's easy to smile back and talk a little. Colin won't be bragging to her about beating the JV team on an iffy call made by their own assistant coach in the last seconds.

She leaves, and the hallway empties. I'm heading out when Coach Smiley appears in the doorway and motions for me to come over.

"Nate Dravus, right? And your partner out there was Lucas Cawley?"

I nod, wondering if he's going to say something about his call.

"Got to say, I was impressed with your play," he says. "So was Coach Varner." He pauses. "We've got you both penciled in for spots on the varsity next year, backing up Colin and Bo. Are you on a club team?"

I shake my head. "We played rec league last spring," I say.

He wags his head back and forth. "Well, yeah, okay. Rec league is better than nothing, but Coach Varner is trying to get as many of our guys working out with Champions as possible. Playing together, growing together—it will make a difference. Next year's team could be special, maybe get Coach Varner that Metro title he deserves. You might talk to your parents."

"I will," I say, my stomach knotting.

When I get home, my parents are waiting in the front room. "That was such a great game," my dad says. Next, my mom goes off on how the last call sucked. "Refs should never decide a game. Never." I think about bringing up Champions, but I don't want to risk spoiling the good vibes.

59

A WEEK GOES BY, AND my dad reminds me to sign up for the spring rec league at the community center. "Sign Lucas up, too," he says.

I tell him I will, but I don't.

Instead, I pore over the Champions website. I watch YouTube videos of their practices, which are highly structured—nothing like Ethan Chan's rec league practices, which is no surprise considering all the coaches are former college players.

The website mainly focuses on the Champions team that takes part in spring and summer tournaments all over the country. Colin and Bo are both on the team, and so is Arthur Jacobson. They call it their Gold Program, and it costs thousands of dollars—no way my parents will pay for that.

I keep digging, though, and discover a Silver Program. No travel, but it costs a lot less, and I'd still have practices three times a week and maybe play in some local tournaments.

My printer makes its normal whirring sound before

producing three pages. I gather the papers and my courage and head downstairs.

My parents are watching *Fauda*, an Israeli series about terrorism that they're hooked on. Mom looks at me, then back to the TV. When the scene shifts, she hits pause.

"Something on your mind?" Dad asks.

"Actually, yeah." I stop.

"So, tell us," Mom says, opening her hands.

I chew on my lip a little before plunging forward. "Instead of the rec league, I want to join Champions."

They look at one another. My dad's eyes turn back to me. "Is that the club you talked about last year?"

I nod, handing him the application. He scans it, and his eyebrows go up. He passes the papers to my mom. Another scan. Another set of raised eyebrows.

My mom speaks. "There are two levels of membership, Nate. Gold and Silver. Which one—"

"Not the Gold," I say quickly. "I'm talking about the Silver program. It's lots cheaper."

They both look at the form again. "It doesn't look like you'd have any games," Mom says. "It's just practice, practice, practice. You'd be okay with that?"

I nod. "Definitely. Practice is what I need."

"One other thing," she says. "This would just be you. We can't pay for Lucas."

"I'll show him the new stuff I learn," I say. "I did that with the JV team until he joined, and it was okay."

"All right, then," Mom says. "Go for it."

Dad points to the paper. "Did you see you need a recommendation from your coach?"

"I'll email him," I say. "I think he'll do it."

"I'm sure he will," my dad says. "I just wasn't sure you'd noticed."

60

IT ISN'T SPRING BREAK OR a holiday, but Amelia comes home that weekend. Another unusual thing—Mom and Dad are always excited when she comes home, but not this time.

Friday after school, she's sitting on the sofa with Mom when I step in the door. She smiles when she sees me, but I can tell she's been crying.

"Bro!" she says, forcing a smile, and she stands and hugs me, which is getting to be normal.

She sits back down while I go into the kitchen, make myself a peanut butter sandwich, and eat it there. Amelia's voice is so soft I can't hear anything she is saying, but I can pick up a few of my mom's words: "always going to be an adjustment . . . finish the year . . . support you whatever you decide."

There's a silence before Amelia climbs the stairs to her room. I finish my sandwich, clean up, and head outside to shoot hoops with Lucas.

I return an hour later and go to my room. Once I'm stretched out on my bed, I try to play a video game on my laptop, but thoughts kept swirling in my head. All my life, Amelia has been golden. Now, though, she's miserable. And me? I've caught the eye of the varsity coach and am signed up for select basketball. Even my grades are better—finally, some As. The world is upside down.

There's a tapping at my door—Amelia.

"You feel like doing something after dinner?" she asks.

"Sure," I say, surprised that she hasn't arranged to see Alice or Eleanor.

We had a good time playing miniature golf over at Interbay, so we go back. A light rain starts falling on the second hole. "You want to hear something funny?" she says as she pulls the hood of her sweatshirt over her head. "At Berkeley, everybody would go inside now. 'It's so cold. It's so rainy,' they'd say. I miss the rain. I never thought I'd say that, but I do."

"You'll get used to being down there," I say as I'm lining up a putt.

"You sound like Mom and Dad." She pauses. "Hey, congrats on your season," she says. "I wish I'd seen that last game."

"Thanks," I say. I know I'm about to brag, but I can't stop myself. "Remember Smiley, Varner's assistant coach? He says Varner has my name down for a spot on next year's varsity."

She exhales loudly. "My coach wants me to transfer so he can give my scholarship to someone new."

She lines up her putt and rolls it in.

"Are you going to leave Berkeley?" I ask.

"I don't know. Mom and Dad don't want me to. They think I can do anything. The truth is, coming back here, going to U Dub or Seattle U and not playing soccer at all sounds like heaven."

We reach the eighteenth hole with the score tied. Again. The eighteenth is tricky—you have to time your putt so it slips through a clown's mouth that opens wide but then snaps closed. My ball arrives just as the mouth shuts. The ball smacks into one of the clown's teeth and rolls back to me. Amelia puts her ball down, waits, then strokes it through the mouth, over a slope, off some bricks, and into the hole—the first hole in one for either of us.

"I win!" she says, her eyes bright.

We're headed back to the pro shop to return the putters and golf balls when Colin, in his mom's SUV, drives by us, with Bo in the passenger seat and some other guys in the back.

"Colin's got his license?" Amelia says.

I nod.

Her eyes narrow. "He's not supposed to have other kids in the car for the first six months."

"Come on, Amelia. You telling me you never drove with your friends when they first got their licenses?"

She half smiles. "Okay, maybe once or twice." She pauses. "What about you? You signed up for driver's ed? The class with that guy on Leary Avenue is good."

I shake my head. "Not yet. I've been so focused on basketball that there's been no time."

"Don't wait too long," she says. "He fills up, and you do not want to have Mom or Dad teach you. Every time I drove with either of them, it was a disaster."

61

MONDAY MORNING, COACH RODRIGUEZ STOPS me in the hall. "I
sent in your recommendation. Great plan. Perfect spot. The
varsity will need somebody to come off the bench to give Colin
and Bo a breather." He pauses. "What about Lucas? He joining,
too?"

"I don't think his family has the money," I say, and the words
feel wrong, as if I'm betraying a secret.

Coach Rodriguez blows out some air. "That's too bad. You
two are a dynamic duo." Then he purses his lips. "We're not
great friends or anything, but I know the director at Champions. Lucas has had a tough road. I'll make a call, see if I can get
him in on a scholarship. Don't say anything to him, though.
This may not fly."

When he says that, my spirits surge. For years, I wanted
nothing to do with Lucas. Now, going to Champions without
him wouldn't feel right.

The next day, Coach Rodriguez stops me in the hall. "I talked to the director," he says, "and explained Lucas's situation. Long story short—they're taking Lucas as a scholarship player."

For a moment I'm excited, but then dread hits me. Coach Rodriguez notices. "What is it?" he says.

"He won't like being the poor kid," I say.

Coach Rodriguez thinks for a moment. "All right," he says at last. "Here's what we'll do. I'll tell Lucas that Champions is my idea. I'll say I know the director, which is true, and that I told him about the two of you, how you're talented but raw and need coaching. All that is true too. If Lucas asks about money—and he might not—I'll tell him that Shilshole High sponsors JV players all the time. He'll think we're sponsoring both of you." Coach Rodriguez stops and looks at me. I wasn't used to an adult working out an elaborate lie, and it must have shown on my face. He smiles and opens his hands. "Not exactly the truth, but who gets hurt?"

62

WE GO TO OUR FIRST Champions practice in mid-March. I eat a small dinner, get a couple of "Good lucks!" and "You'll do great!" from my parents, and leave.

Lucas is standing by his shed, waiting for me, Megan at his side.

"Give me a second," he says once I cross the street. I wait as he goes to the shed and opens the door. Bill is inside. "Hello, Nate," he calls out.

"Hello," I shout back.

Megan is sitting on her ladder, Lucas standing next to her, pointing to her watch, showing her when he'll be back. She nods, and we're off.

All Seattle high school kids get free bus passes. It's a short walk to the RapidRide D stop on Fifteenth Avenue. Neither of us talks at all. I can tell he's nervous, which makes me feel better about the condition of my stomach.

The bus takes us across the Ballard Bridge and past the

driving range, and we reach our stop in front of the animal shelter. We can hear dogs howling as we walk down West Wheeler toward the gym.

We wait a beat before climbing the steps and pushing open the gym doors. Once inside, I look around, getting my bearings. There are three full-size courts. The middle court is empty, but the court to the left is alive with about twenty guys shooting around. They're all wearing either red or blue Champions jerseys with a number on the back. On the wall above one of the hoops is a sign that reads Silver.

That's us.

I glance over to the court to the right, which has ten or twelve guys on it. The sign there reads Gold. I spot Colin, then catch Bo's eye and give him a half wave, but get nothing back.

Lucas starts toward the Silver court, and I follow. We stand off to the side, wondering what to do until a tall Black woman wearing a blue T-shirt that reads COACH spots us and comes over.

"You the new guys?" she asks.

"Yeah," Lucas says.

"I'm Gwen Dawson," she says, "but from now on you just call me Coach Dawson. Since you're white boys, I'm guessing you're glad that a Black person will be teaching you basketball but disappointed that the Black person is a female. So, listen up. I was a starter at UW for two years until I tore my ACL. Got a job as a cop when I graduated, but I miss hoops, so I do this gig in my spare time. I can't jump or run worth crap anymore, but if you pay attention to me, you'll get better. You don't, and you won't."

We both nod a bunch.

"We have three sessions per week—Monday, Wednesday, and Thursday," she goes on. "Every session starts with the basics—dribbling, passing, shooting. Things you think you know how to do, but don't. The second half emphasizes one skill. This week it's the pick-and-roll." She stops and hands a reversible jersey to me and another one to Lucas. "Put it on, red showing, and wear it every time. Now get out there and warm up. We start in three minutes."

After she turns and walks away, I peel off my T-shirt and pull the jersey over my head while Lucas does the same. My number is 3; his is 7.

We join other guys shooting at a side hoop—including Tony Nevin. "I didn't know you came here," I say.

"This is my second time," he says. "Varner is pushing it hard."

"Anybody else from JV joining?" I ask.

"Patrick Colligan might stick with tennis, but Bryce Chambers, the tight end on the football team, says he's going to sign up after spring football. Flynn Westwood is going to join in the summer, and probably other guys will, too."

Lucas and I toss up a few shots before Coach Dawson blows her whistle and calls everybody to her for instructions.

The session starts with passing drills. I think my technique is fine, but Coach Dawson doesn't like my accuracy. She doesn't bother with names, mine or anybody else's. I'm Three. "Put it on the numbers, Three!" she barks. "You hit a teammate in rhythm, and the shot that goes up, goes in. If he's not in rhythm, it's going to be off the front rim, the back rim, or an airball. The pass makes the shot."

After she finishes ripping into the way I pass the ball, she tears into how I catch it. "You're letting the ball get into you. Those hands aren't strong enough. Buy yourself some hand grippers and use them."

The passing drills go on and on. A couple of times I look over at Bo and Colin and the other guys on the Gold court. They have two coaches—Tijuan Angelo, a six-six Black guy who played college ball in Iowa, and Don LaChapelle, a white guy around six feet, who is a magician with the ball.

The shriek of a whistle brings everyone to a stop. I look around to find Coach Dawson in my face. "Hey, Three, you want to pull up a chair and watch those guys?"

"What?" I mumble.

Her eyes widen. "I said, *Do you want to watch them?* Because if you do, then get off my court. But if you're staying here, I want your attention *here.*"

"Yes, ma'am."

"I'm not ma'am. I'm Coach."

"Yes, Coach."

The only sound is the squeaking of sneakers from the other court.

Coach Dawson's eyes stay on me. "All right. Since I've got your attention, we'll work on the screen-and-roll. Three, you and Seven take the court. You can show us how it's done."

The other guys move to the side. "I'll play defense," Coach

Dawson barks. "I'm sure you two can run circles around a *girl* with bad knees."

I have the ball up top, with Coach Dawson guarding me. Lucas comes up and sets the screen. I dribble; she stays with me. Lucas rolls to the hoop, and I make a good pass, but she deflects it.

She retrieves the ball and slaps it hard. "Okay. Seven did set a screen and he did roll, but everything else he did was wrong."

For the rest of that session Coach Dawson explains how to create the proper separation, how to get the best angle, when to sneak in a little nudge.

After that, using a couple of rollaway hoops that had been pushed up against the wall, we go two-on-two, the blue shirts staying put while the reds rotate every four minutes. "I want to see the pick-and-roll!" Dawson hollers.

We are the new guys, but we hold our own. As game follows game, the other guys get lazy or bored, or both. Once that happens, we take it to them, stifling them on defense and lighting them up when we have the ball, easily winning the last two matchups.

The whistle blows, ending the session. Lucas and I retrieve our T-shirts and head to the bus stop.

"Bad," Coach Dawson says as we leave, "but not horrible."

63

THE NEXT MONDAY, BO AND Colin come over while I'm warming up. They've just returned from a tournament in Palm Springs, and they tell me about the resort hotel with a pool and a hot tub and dozens of beautiful girls wandering around in bikinis. They make sure I see their swag, too—gym bags and water bottles, T-shirts and sweatpants.

When they return to the Gold court, Coach Dawson slides over. "Those two started for the varsity at your high school, right? And you and Number Seven played JV?"

"Yeah," I say, surprised. "How did you know that?"

"I know lots of things." She pauses. "I suppose they've been doing that to you for a while?"

"Doing what?"

"Rubbing your nose in it."

"No big deal," I say. "I'm okay with it."

She snorts. "You okay if they keep doing it?"

She found a sore spot; I look her in the eyes. "No."

Coach Dawson smiles. "Glad to hear it." She looks over her shoulder and nods toward Lucas. "Your friend over there? Seven? He plays like a junkyard dog. Fifty-fifty balls? He's getting them. Charges? He's taking them. You've got some of his mangy-dog attitude. Get more, add it to that silky-smooth shot, and next year you could be rubbing their noses in it."

The fantasy Lucas and I had of forcing those two to the bench? Coach Dawson isn't the kind to blow smoke. If she thinks we have a chance, then we have a chance.

64

AMELIA HAD SAID THAT SHE was coming home for spring break in April, but toward the end of March she calls to say that her coach wants her to stay and play in a tournament in Berkeley.

"That's good, isn't it?" I say to her when it's my turn on the phone. "He wants you around."

"I think it might be my last chance to show him I can play," she says.

"You can play, Amelia," I say. "You're the best."

She scoffs at that. "Not here, Bro. Not on this team."

We talk a little longer before she disconnects. When I bring my mom's phone down to her, she's sitting at the kitchen table with my dad, drinking coffee, both looking sad.

"They can't take her scholarship away, can they?" I ask. "Not if her grades are good?"

Mom opens her hands. "Technically, no. But if they stick her at the end of the bench and never play her . . ." Mom's voice trails off.

Dad jumps in. "Nate, we're thinking of flying down to visit her for a few days over spring break. All of us being there to support her, cheer her up. Sound good?"

"Sure," I say. "No problem."

65

THE LAST DAY OF MARCH is challenge day at Champions. It's something they do every month, so for the other guys it's ho-hum, but it's new to me and Lucas. The format is simple: win, and you move up a court; lose, and you go down a court.

Before tip-off, Coach Dawson calls the Silver players to her. "Listen," she says in a low voice. "Those guys over there? They fly around the country playing in fancy tournaments and staying at fancy hotels, but all that means is that their parents are rich. Okay, so you're homeboys. So what? You can beat them."

Since Lucas and I are new guys, our team starts at the bottom, on court three. We get Tony Nevin on our team, because he's new, and two other decent players, Jonathan Forester and Colton Casey.

Colin and Bo and Arthur Jacobson are on court one teamed with two starters from Bishop Blanchet High: Charles Chenier, who can really sky, and Manny Suarez, a stocky guy with a game a lot like Bo's. I nudge Lucas and motion toward court one. "That's where we need to get," I say.

He points at the team we're going to play. "We got to beat these guys first," he says, and he's right. Looking ahead is a sure way to lose.

The game starts badly. After they control the opening tip, I back off my guy, Max Reed, as he dribbles into front court. Reed's eyes are scanning the court, and I'm trying to anticipate where his pass is headed, when he unexpectedly lets fly a twenty-five-footer that hits nothing but net. He pumps his fist, grinning, and his teammates grin back at him as they drop back on defense. Twenty seconds later, after Nevin misses a baby hook, Reed lets fly another three-pointer, this time from the left corner. Another swish.

As it turns out, those two triples are the worst thing that could have happened to them. A minute into the game, they relax, overconfident.

We score on our next possession when I thread the needle with a bounce pass to Lucas on a backdoor play. After a turn-over, Nevin banks in a turnaround jumper. A miss by Reed leads to a fast break hoop by Lucas, and a steal leads to another breakaway hoop for me. And that's how it goes. Instead of them thrashing us, we thrash them.

A whistle blows, and we move up to court two to take on the second-string guys from the Gold squad. I don't know how badly Colin and those guys beat this team, but from the looks on their faces, it was a wipeout, which is great for us because they are lifeless at the start, and we make them even more miserable.

I say "we," but mainly it's Lucas. Coach Dawson is the ref on the middle court, and maybe she lets a few things go that are fouls, but she calls it the same way for both teams. Early in the game Lucas makes a steal and drives for a lay-in. Nevin misses a shot, but Lucas gets the rebound and scores the putback. I drop in a three-pointer. The other two guys on our team, Forester and Casey, each get a hoop. It's our defense, though, that is key. We roll over them, winning by ten and sending them to court three while we move up to court one to take on the first-string Gold team.

After a five-minute break, it's game on.

66

WHEN COLIN COMES ON THE court and sees Lucas heading to match up with him, he gets a *not you again!* look on his face. Lucas's expression is snake cold.

We're playing a thirty-minute, running clock. Tijuan Angelo, the head coach of the Gold team, is the ref. Everybody says he's a fair guy, and I hope it's true.

For the first seven minutes or so, both teams play straight up man-to-man. Colin is their point guard, their leader, but Lucas's defense stymies him. Colin is tentative with his shot and his passes, and with him out of sorts, their entire team is out of sorts.

Not us, though. Nevin is tough on the boards, and so are Casey and Forester, so we hold our own there. Lucas banks in a couple of jumpers; I hit a long three. When the water break comes at the thirteen-minute mark, we're up by seven, and I'm thinking we're going to pull it off.

After the break, they go into what I learn later is the triangle offense. Colin is up top, Bo is on the wing, Charles on the post. The three set screens for one another, make back cuts, do lobs over the top. If nothing works, they form a triangle on the other side using their other two guys, Jacobson and Manny Suarez, and go at us again.

On defense, they switch to a matchup zone. When either Lucas or I get the ball, they trap us, putting the pressure on Nevin or Forester or Casey to score. Those guys try, but shots clank off the rim.

With five minutes left, they take their first lead and—there's no other word for it—I panic. I shoot when I shouldn't; I dribble too much; I try for steals instead of playing solid defense. It's not just me, it's all of us. Everybody is trying, but we stop playing as a team.

They win by nine.

After we shake hands, Lucas and I head for the exit, shoulders slumped. We're about out the door when Coach Angelo calls our names. "Hold up a second," he says.

He talks to Coach Dawson before coming over to us. "Don't get down on yourselves," he says. "Every one of those guys has been here for at least a year, you've been here a month, and you still had them on the ropes there. That triangle offense is tough to defend if you've never seen it. That's the offense the Bulls ran during Michael Jordan's time. Did you know that?"

I shake my head and so does Lucas.

"Watch the YouTube videos," Coach Angelo says. "We use it a lot here, and Coach Varner is going to put it in next year."

"I will," I say.

"I need to get going," Lucas says, and I know he's thinking about Megan.

"Right," Coach Angelo says. "So let me get to it. A couple of our regular Gold team guys are going on vacation, so we've got spots open for the Nooksack Spring Break Challenge in Whatcom County this Saturday. You are my first choice as replacements—no cost, and we'll get you there in our van. It's all over in a single day, and you'll get a swag bag full of goodies. Talk to your parents and see what they say."

On the bus ride home, I work on Lucas. "Megan will be fine," I tell him. "She's on her own every day at school, and Bill will be around."

"You could go without me," he says. "It doesn't have to be both of us."

"Who would I hang out with?" I say. "And we're a team, right? It'll be great."

67

WHEN I STEP INSIDE MY house, my parents are drinking wine and watching another episode of *Fauda*. I go upstairs, shower, and then return to the living room.

"I got some news," I say, and I tell them about Nooksack.

When I finish, my mom puts down her wineglass. "Nate, we're leaving Friday to visit Amelia in Berkeley," she says. "You know that."

I'd totally forgotten.

"I don't want to go," I say.

Dad gives me a disgusted look. "We bought your ticket. You're going. End of discussion."

I swallow. "I'll pay you back."

My parents look at one another. "The Nooksack Spring Break Challenge?" Dad says. "Seriously? You want to skip a trip to Berkeley to see your sister, who could use your support, because the Nooksack Spring Break Challenge is more important?"

"What about support for me?" I say, feeling the anger rise.

"It's always Amelia this and Amelia that. What about my chance to do something?"

"Nate," my mother says, "that's not fair. We've always—"

"No, you haven't," I say. "You thought the whole basketball thing was a waste until you saw me play against the varsity. And that didn't stick, because you want me to give up a chance to play against top competition to go to Berkeley when I'll just be in the way, and you know it."

"You won't be in the way," Dad says.

"Yes, I will. You want to talk to Amelia about her future and all that, so you'll find some reason to send me off somewhere for a couple of hours, and you'll wish I was gone longer. It'll be better if I'm not there."

The room goes quiet. "Give us some time to think about it," Mom says. "And you think about it, too. All of us are worked up right now."

I start to my room, then turn back. "They want Lucas to play, too," I say, "but he won't go if I don't go. You're always saying that he—"

"Enough," my dad says. "This is about our family. It's not about Lucas."

"Fine," I say, and I do go upstairs, but I can't sleep. I open my computer and read an email from Coach Angelo giving details about the Nooksack tournament. After I finish, I close my computer and stare at the ceiling, going over the argument I'd had with my parents, wishing I'd said this or that. It's almost eleven when I hear Lucas outside, shooting hoops in the moonlight.

68

IN THE MORNING, WHEN I go downstairs, my dad gets right to it. "You still want to go to Nooksack?" he asks.

"Yeah," I say, "I do."

"All right then, you can go," he says. "We'll explain to Amelia; she'll understand."

Mom jumps in. "But you call me between games. If I don't answer, leave a message. Once you get back to Seattle—no matter how late—call again. Understood?"

I nod.

My dad looks at the wall clock. "We're going in early today, but we'll be back early, too. Dinner at Sen Noodle Bar sound good? Our flight leaves at nine."

I eat breakfast and go outside. I'd won the argument, but I don't feel like celebrating. I look across the street and see Lucas with Megan. She is completely relaxed with him, at peace. Being that important to somebody—it's a great thing, but it's an awful thing, too.

We stand with Megan until her bus picks her up. As we walk to school, I give Lucas the details about Nooksack. I half expect him to say he's not going, but he doesn't. "We'd better play," he says. "I don't want to sit."

I'm in a daze in my classes. At lunch, I look up to see Hanna and Colin standing in front of me. "A bunch of us are going to Golden Gardens after school," Hanna says. "It'll be cold, but first day of break we got to do something. Why don't you come?"

I shake my head. "I can't," I say.

"All work and no play makes Jack a dull boy," Colin says, his eyes wide and his voice menacing. After a moment, his face returns to normal. "Jack Nicholson in *The Shining*," he says. "You've seen the movie, right?"

I know who Jack Nicholson is, but I'd never seen any of his movies. "Yeah, I've seen it," I say.

Colin scoffs at that, then tugs on Hanna's arm. "Let's get some food."

"If you change your mind," Hanna says as she's walking away, "we'll be on the field by the duck ponds."

After school, I've just started shooting around with Lucas when my dad's car pulls up in front of the house and my parents get out. My dad motions with his head for me to come inside.

"See you tomorrow morning," I say to Lucas.

Twenty minutes later, we are at the Sen Noodle Bar on Market. I like the food, but at four thirty in the afternoon I'm not that hungry.

Back home, I go up to my room to study, knowing they're

leaving soon. I hear them rustling about, then hear them carrying luggage to the car. My dad knocks, comes in, ruffles my hair. "Good luck with the tournament," he says.

He leaves, and my mom comes in.

She sits on my bed, which I don't like. Then she pats the spot next to her, wanting me to get up from my desk and sit next to her, which I like even less.

"Now listen to me, Nate," she says once we're side by side. "Maybe it sometimes seems that we've given more attention to—"

"It's okay, Mom," I say, not liking where she's going. "Really. Everything is okay."

"You sure? Talking about—"

"I'm sure, Mom. Really. There's nothing to talk about."

She stares at me, and I force myself to hold her gaze. Then she sighs and kisses me on the forehead. "All right, Y chromosome. I'll leave you alone. But remember to call tomorrow, and good luck! Come back with your shield—or on it."

69

WHEN I STEP OUTSIDE THE next morning, Lucas is waiting at the curb, his eyes tense. "This'll be good," I say, giving him a fist bump. "We're going to kick some Nooksack butt."

The team van pulls up right at seven. As we get on, a couple of guys nod, but most—including Colin and Bo—have their eyes closed, either sleeping or trying to.

The drive to the Whatcom County rec center takes almost two hours. I try to sleep, but I'm too nervous. Sometimes I picture myself making the shot to win the tournament title. Other times I imagine a screwup so colossal—passing the ball to a guy on the other team or shooting at the wrong basket— that I single-handedly blow the tournament.

When we arrive, Coach Angelo leads us to a locker room that is so old, all the wooden rafters are exposed. The words *Champions Academy* are written on pieces of tape attached to a dozen lockers.

Coach tosses uniforms to Lucas and me. I'm so pumped that

I nearly put my jersey on backwards. Lucas's eyes are as lit up as mine.

As they dress, Bo and Colin and the other guys talk about an upcoming tournament. "You two playing in Tahoe?" Colin asks.

"No," I say as I finish lacing my shoes. "Just this tournament."

"Too bad," Bo puts in. "The best California teams will be there, so the games are great. Afterward, it's jet skiing on the lake. It's a thousand times better than this tournament."

Coach Angelo comes in and claps his hands. "Hustle it up, Champions. First game in thirty."

Taking the court feels strange. In my mind, I'd built up the tournaments until they had become as big as the Final Four. Now I'm finally playing in one, and it's just guys playing ball in an empty gym.

Bo and Colin start at guard, and I sit next to Lucas on the bench. The Fairhaven Panthers are ready to play, but Colin and Bo are sleepwalkers, going through the motions as Fairhaven builds a lead.

I fidget on the bench all through the first quarter. When Bo and Colin start the second quarter, Lucas gives me a *Why are we here?* look. Coach Angelo had promised we'd get some playing time. How much was *some*? I didn't know.

The team plays better for a while, but then Fairhaven scores seven straight on two lay-ins off turnovers and a three-pointer from the corner. As the triple drops through the net, Coach Angelo jumps to his feet to call time. He looks at me and Lucas and gives us the nod. We check in at the scorer's table and make it back to the huddle in time to hear him say, "Let's see some fire out there!"

As I take my position on the court, instead of fire, I feel chill. *These guys are too good for me*, I think. *I don't belong.* I look at Lucas and see no fear, just his don't-mess-with-me look.

Lucas picks up his guy at half-court, so I do the same. The other guys—Chenier, Jacobson, Suarez—follow our lead. Everybody contests shots, crashes the boards, dives for loose balls.

Once we ratchet up the defensive intensity, Fairhaven starts shooting bricks. Nobody on our team catches fire, but we make a decent percentage. When Charles knocks down a jumper from the free throw line just before the end of the half, Fairhaven's lead is a single point.

70

COACH ANGELO STARTS COLIN AND Bo in the third quarter. "See how those two played?" he says to them, nodding in our direction. "How about you guys show me that effort? You're Gold, remember?"

Bo hangs his head, but Colin scowls as he heads onto the court. Coach Angelo's dissing works, though, as they both play hard for the first half of the third quarter, pulling Champions ahead by five. With the lead, Colin reverts to playing relaxed defense, and Bo follows him because that's what Bo does. Fairhaven goes on a 7–0 run to take back the lead.

With two minutes left in the third quarter, Colin, without making a single pass, launches a shot from beyond the top of the key. It bricks off the back iron, the rebound caroming right to the Fairhaven point guard. Immediately he's off, leading a two-on-one fast break that ends with an easy lay-in. Coach Angelo jumps to his feet. "Time out! Time out!" he hollers, and then he turns and points his long finger first to Lucas and then to me. "Check in."

We play tough defense, pumping up our whole team. I start working the high screen-and-roll with Charles, and Fairhaven can't defend it. If they go under the screen, I knock down the open jumper. If they go over it, Charles Chenier rolls to the hoop for a layup or makes a quick pass to Lucas or Manny Suarez for a short jump shot. Jacobson is there for offensive rebounds. When the Fairhaven coach calls time midway through the fourth quarter, we're up by six.

That's when we get the cold water in the face.

Coach takes us out.

My eyes must have shown my shock. "Fresh legs," he says, looking from me to Lucas. "You two did great, now these guys will close the door."

We take seats at the end of the bench and watch. Instead of closing the door, Colin and Bo swing it wide-open. A drive by Fairhaven's forward cuts the lead to four with 3:21 left in the game. Bo rims out a jump shot, and Fairhaven responds with a floater from the foul line, cutting the lead to two. After a couple of misses by both teams, Fairhaven's point guard drives right by Colin for a lay-in, tying the game with twenty seconds on the clock.

Coach Angelo calls his last time-out. He looks down the bench at Lucas and me. He wants to put us back in—I can feel it, but we're not Gold players, not on the travel team. In Tahoe and all the other tournaments, it'll be Colin and Bo.

"Check in, both of you," he says, and we're up and headed to the scorer's table. Seconds later I'm standing next to Coach Angelo as he diagrams a play. "They're going to be looking for that high screen-and-roll. Instead, we're going to—"

As I listen, I can feel Bo and Colin behind me, feel their anger. "Win this game!" Coach Angelo hollers as he finishes.

Lucas inbounds to me, and I dribble slowly into front court, letting time tick away. With eight seconds left, I drive the lane, just as Coach Angelo drew it up. Two Fairhaven guys converge on me. Lucas finds the open space, spotting up fifteen feet out. I feed him a bounce pass, just the way Coach Dawson taught me. He catches it and in one motion rises into the air. The shot arcs high and nestles through.

Guys crowd around Lucas, grabbing and shaking him, and then grabbing and shaking me. Even Colin and Bo join in, sort of. Coach Angelo gives us both knuckle bumps as he says a single word: "Clutch."

71

I'M SO AMPED I WANT to be back on the court right away, but our next game isn't until one. We return to the locker room, where Coach LaChapelle collects everybody's sweaty jerseys—we get a fresh jersey for every game—and hands each of us a swag bag containing Nooksack sweatpants, a Nooksack sweatshirt, and Nooksack flip-flops. "Don't wear your game shoes outside," he says. "They don't want dirt all over their floors."

The last thing we get is a cardboard box containing a giant burrito, a banana, an Amazing Mango, and a package of chocolate chip cookies. We pull on the sweatpants and sweatshirt, trade our shoes for the flip-flops, and head out.

It had been cloudy in the early morning, but now the sun is shining in a blue sky dotted with puffy white clouds. We sit on the main steps and dig into the food. The burrito, the mango juice, and the banana taste great. After gobbling down the chocolate chip cookies, I remember to call my mom. No answer, so I leave a voicemail. "All good here. Say hello to Amelia."

We throw our garbage into a trash can and look at each other. The next game is still over an hour away. "You want to go find the Nooksack River?" I ask.

Lucas shakes his head. "I'm good right here."

"Come on," I say. "All we've got to do is walk downhill and we'll hit it. It can't be far. I don't want to just sit."

With that, I start off, and he follows. As we cross the rec center's soccer field, we hear a distant burbling that grows louder and louder. Opposite the field, we come upon a trail that works its way through some trees and bushes, and after about a hundred winding yards, we're standing on the banks of the Nooksack.

Because of the spring snowmelt in the mountains, the current is strong. We find a trail and hike along the riverbank until the trail ends at a spot where the river is wide and flat, though still moving fast. We skip stones for a while, arguing about whose rock skips the most.

We're there ten minutes when we hear rustling as Colin and Bo come into the clearing. "What are you guys doing?" Colin asks.

"Just kicking around," I say. "We followed that trail, but it ends here." I don't know why, but I'm embarrassed to admit we'd been skipping rocks.

"I doubt the trail ends," Bo says. "I bet it picks up through there."

He walks toward a small opening between some scrubby bushes, and we follow. Sure enough, the trail does start up again, though it's narrower and muddier, not easy going in flip-flops.

We walk slowly, pushing stray branches aside and jumping over a few wet spots, when we come upon two canoes that have been flipped over to keep rainwater out.

"Anybody else thinking what I'm thinking?" Colin asks, his eyes bright.

"What?" I say, not understanding.

Bo and Lucas look puzzled too.

Colin points toward the river. "A little boat ride," he says.

"You want to steal the canoes?" I say in disbelief.

"We're not stealing them," Colin says. "We're *borrowing* them. When we're done, we'll carry them back here. No one will know they've been gone." He flips one canoe over, and then the other. "These are nice, and they left the paddles," he says. "There are even life jackets."

"I don't know," Bo says.

I look at Lucas and can tell he wants no part of this. I give my head a shake.

"Don't be such wusses," Colin says. "We've got an hour before our next game. What else are we going to do? And the river is wide-open."

"It's wide-open here, but how do you know there will be a place to land them down there?" I ask. "What if we end up going down the river for miles?"

Colin points back to where we'd come from. "There have been places all along the river where it'd be easy to land," he says.

"That doesn't mean there will be more," I say.

Colin sighs. "All right, ladies. Let's go check."

We follow the trail as it bends to the right, the river growing narrower, making the current faster. Past that section—which is about the length of two basketball courts—the river widens again. "See," Colin says, pointing to a long, flat section of riverbank. "It'll be a cinch to land there. No bushes, no trees. We carry the canoes back, and no one ever knows."

On the hike back to the canoes, Colin and Bo fall behind for a while, talking quietly and laughing. I look out at the water in the one narrow spot. It's not white water, but it's close. My parents had taken me river rafting once. "Every river has its secrets," the guide had said.

72

WHEN WE REACH THE CANOES, Colin takes charge. "You and Lucas go first, and we'll follow."

"Shouldn't you go first?" I say. "You know more about this."

"That's why you should go first," he says. "We can help you if you have trouble—which you won't."

"I don't want to get these clothes wet," I say.

"You're not going to get wet," Colin says. "You're worrying about nothing."

I ignore him and strip down to my gym shorts and my T-shirt, putting my sweatshirt and sweatpants up on the bank. Lucas does the same.

Colin maneuvers the first canoe so that the bow is barely in the water. Lucas climbs in, the boat rocking as he creeps to the front seat. Once he's settled, I step in, doing my best to keep the canoe from rocking. The life jackets are on the shore, about twenty feet away. I meant to grab them, but now it's too late.

"Ready . . ." Colin says, "set . . . go!"

He gives the canoe a hard push. My heart jumps as I feel the current grab us, pulling us downstream. I paddle fast, working the canoe away from the riverbank. When we reach open water, I look back over my shoulder. The second canoe is still sitting on the bank, and I don't see Colin or Bo. What are they doing?

Then I spot them, jogging carefully along the trail in their flip-flops, pointing at us and laughing, as our canoe, starting to turn this way and that, enters the narrow section of fast water.

I don't have time to be angry, because our canoe gets caught in an eddy and does a 360. From the bank, I hear a laughing scream. "Watch out!"

The current is taking us straight toward a group of boulders that are just above the surface. "Left!" I scream to Lucas. "Left."

Maybe he hears me, maybe he doesn't. I try to use the paddle to steer clear, but the river has its own plan, pulling us toward the rocks.

Suddenly the Nooksack disappears from under us. We drop what feels like thirty feet but is probably a yard. Then the river has us again. To the left, fifty yards away, is calmer water. I paddle toward it . . . closer . . . closer.

The boulder must have been entirely under the water because I never see it. I hear the collision, though, and see the canoe tilt, and watch as Lucas is thrown out. A fraction of a second later, I'm out too, struggling to raise my head above the swirling water, the river pushing me right, then left, as if I were a leaf.

I drive down with my hands, getting my head above water long enough to fill my lungs with air. I look, and there it is, just ten yards away—calm water and then the riverbank. I put my head down and swim. One stroke . . . two strokes . . . three . . . four . . . five. The current isn't pushing me anymore; the surging violent water is behind me. I put my feet down and touch bottom.

I'm safe.

I stand for a minute or two, letting the pounding of my heart slow as the water swirls around my legs. Then I wade the last yards through shallow water until I'm up on the riverbank. Within seconds, Colin and Bo burst out of the trail and into view, their eyes bright, grins on their faces.

My teeth start chattering, making it hard to talk. "Big joke," I manage.

"Come on. You had fun. Admit it," Colin says as he takes off his sweatshirt and gives it to me.

As I peel off my T-shirt and pull the sweatshirt on, I look back at the river. The canoe is about fifty yards away, upside down, on the opposite bank.

"Where'd Lucas end up?" I ask as I move into the sunlight for more warmth, my teeth not chattering quite as much.

"We lost him when he went around that bend," Bo says. "He'll be on the bank just past that tree hanging over the water."

Colin looks out. "How are we going to get that canoe back over here?" he says.

"This was your idea," I snap. "You figure it out."

"Okay, okay, I'm sorry," he says, his grin gone. "We didn't

think you'd flip the boat. Stay in the sun, and you'll dry off in a few minutes."

I shake my head. "Let's just find Lucas and get out of here." I stand and start downriver.

It's hard getting around the tree that's hanging out over the water, but we manage. When we reach the open riverbank we'd scouted earlier, I turn back to Colin and Bo. "This is where he was headed, right?"

"Yeah," Colin says. "He's got to be around here."

"Lucas!" I call.

I look down the river. Just past where we are, the river is moving fast again. A sick feeling comes over me.

"He must be a little farther down," Bo says.

We walk, silent, looking, until we come to the next clearing.

"Is he messing with us?" Colin says, nervous.

"Lucas," I call. "Lucas!"

And then we're all moving in random directions, up and down the riverbank, shouting more and more, our voices louder and louder.

"Lucas!"

"Lucas!"

"Lucas!"

73

I STAY BY THE RIVER, searching, while Colin and Bo race back to the gym to get help. For a while I don't think anyone is coming, but then suddenly all the guys from all the teams are running along the bank, calling, *"Lucas, Lucas, Lucas."* Sirens wail in the distance, coming closer with every second.

Then I hear "Here! Over here!" in a frantic voice. A tall kid wearing a maroon jersey with 45 on the back is waving his arms wildly. He's back upriver, not too far from the spot where I came out.

I try to run, but the stupid flip-flops cause me to stumble. I get up, stumble again. I follow Number 45's eyes and see Lucas— face down, arms out like drowned people in the movies—fifteen feet from solid earth and life.

Number 45 has hold of Lucas's shirt. As he's pulling him to the riverbank, a coach from one of the other teams races down into the river to help. Once the two of them have pulled Lucas to land, the coach flips Lucas over to drain the water out of his lungs before laying him on his back and pushing up and down on his chest. Within minutes, two medics appear and take over. I keep waiting to hear Lucas cough, splutter, gasp, and come back to life. It has to happen. It just has to.

74

SOMEBODY BRINGS MY GYM BAG. I pull my jeans over my half-dry shorts and put on socks and shoes. A cop drives me to the Whatcom County police department, where a detective named Strauss leads me down a hallway and into a small room. On the way, I see Colin in one room and Bo in another. Detective Strauss sits me down and shoves a bottle of water at me.

"You okay?" he asks, anger in his voice.

"I'm okay," I say.

"All right," he says. "Go slow and tell me everything that happened."

He lets me talk, straight through, without interrupting. I hold the water in front of me and stare at the label as I talk, my throat thick, my chest tight. I want to stop and drink some of the water, but I don't deserve to stop, so I keep going. When I finish, I look up, and he's staring at me—I can still feel his eyes. "There were life jackets, right?" he says.

I nod.

"Did you think about wearing them?"

"I remembered them after we got in the canoe, but by then everything was ready, so we just went."

"You just went," he says. "You just went into a river without life jackets even though they were right there."

I don't answer.

He leans forward and taps his pencil on the desk. "Were you drinking? Doing drugs?"

"No. Nothing like that."

More pencil tapping. He doesn't believe me, which I get. When guys our age screw up, it's almost always drugs or booze or both.

"You want to rethink that answer?" he says. "Because there'll be a toxicology report. It'd be better if the truth came out now."

"We didn't drink or do drugs," I say. "It was all basketball."

75

DETECTIVE STRAUSS LEAVES THE ROOM for fifteen or twenty minutes. When he comes back, he makes me tell him everything a second time. He goes away, comes back, and makes me go through everything a third time. Finally, he takes down my name, address, and cell number and lets me go. Bo's father has driven up, and he gives me a ride back. No one speaks.

As Bo's father drives toward Seattle, I know that Bill or Richard or Lucas's mom or maybe all of them are driving to Whatcom County to identify Lucas's body. Would they bring Megan with them? That would be terrible, but she wouldn't want to be left in Seattle, either.

When the SUV finally pulls up in front of my house, I nod to Bo and Colin and thank Bo's father. It's nine o'clock when I step inside my front door. I flop down on the sofa and listen to the hum of the refrigerator.

I hadn't called my parents since leaving the message on my mom's phone after our morning game. I have this idea that I won't have to tell them about Lucas, that somehow, they'll hear. But how? Some kid drowning on the Nooksack River in Washington wouldn't be headline news in California. Besides, if my parents knew, they'd have phoned. I lay my phone on the cushion, stare at it for a while, then make the call.

My mom answers, her voice cheery. "How did you do? How did the games go?"

This makes no sense, but I describe the first game and how we'd come from behind and won because of Lucas and me.

"That sounds so exciting," she says. "I wish we could have been there. Hopefully one of the parents filmed it."

"Probably," I mumble. I'm working up the courage to tell her about Lucas when she cuts me off.

"Let me get your dad. And Amelia wants to say hello, too."

Seconds later my dad is on the line. While I'm listening to myself again describe the last minute of the game, all I see is Lucas, face down in the water, arms out.

After that it's Amelia's turn. "What's up, Bro?" she says. My throat is so tight I can't talk. Seconds go by. "Nate? You there?"

"Lucas is dead," I blurt out.

"What did you say?"

"Lucas. He's dead."

Amelia's voice is both scared and angry. "Nate, if this is a joke, it's not funny."

"He drowned in the Nooksack River."

AFTER

1

MY PARENTS BOOK THE FIRST available flight back to Seattle. It's nearly three in the morning when the front door opens, but I'm awake. I hear them rustling around, talking in low voices. I pull sweatpants and a sweatshirt over my pajamas and head downstairs.

In the kitchen, my mom and dad are sitting across the table from one another, each holding a glass of wine. When my mom sees me, she starts toward me. I step to the side, keeping a kitchen chair between her and me. I don't want a hug. Why should anybody feel sorry for me?

I tell what happened again. Details make things real, and I don't want things to be real, so I rush. When I finish, there's silence. "We all should try to get some sleep," my dad says. He comes over and squeezes my shoulder. When I stand, my mom hugs me before I have a chance to move away.

I don't think I'll sleep, but when I wake up, it's after ten. I go to the window and look out across the street. Lucas's house is dark, but the door to the shed is open. I can just make out the rhythmic sound of a handsaw—Bill making flower box number six thousand.

I kill time brushing my teeth and combing my hair—I don't want to go downstairs. When I finally do, my dad and mom are drinking coffee and talking, but they stop when they see me. "I can scramble up some eggs if you want," my mom says, her eyes red.

The night before, I didn't think I'd ever eat again, but I'm starving. "That would be good," I say. "Thanks."

The first three or four mouthfuls taste great, but after that, the eggs gross me out. Slimy, yellow unborn chickens.

I stand. "I should go see Bill," I say.

"You want me to go with you?" my dad asks.

I shake my head.

A couple minutes later I'm outside Bill's shed, peering in. He has a board laid out across two sawhorses, and his arm is going back and forth. Megan sits motionless on a stool across from him.

Bill notices me and stops sawing. "Nate," he says, and smiles. Then his head falls a little to the side, his shoulders slump, and the smile disappears.

I feel wobbly, as if I'm walking on the deck of a ship in a storm. I wait for him to ask me questions, but he stays silent. I finally mumble something about it being an accident and not understanding how it happened.

When I stop, he walks over and squeezes my shoulder the same way my dad had. "You were a good friend," he says. After he loosens his grip, he returns to the sawhorses, and once again his arm goes back and forth, back and forth. I watch for a moment and then nod goodbye to Megan. Her eyes are empty, as if everything behind them has been sucked out.

I'm heading back to my house when my phone vibrates—a text message from Hanna. I open it and see row after row of sad faces. I text sad faces back to her, rows and rows of them.

☹ ☹ ☹ ☹ ☹ ☹ ☹ ☹ ☹
☹ ☹ ☹ ☹ ☹ ☹ ☹ ☹ ☹
☹ ☹ ☹ ☹ ☹ ☹ ☹ ☹ ☹
☹ ☹ ☹ ☹ ☹ ☹ ☹ ☹ ☹
☹ ☹ ☹ ☹ ☹ ☹ ☹ ☹ ☹

x x x

Hey Lucas—

I bet you're wondering why I'm writing to you, because I'm wondering the same thing—so here goes.

Right after Nooksack, my parents wanted me to talk to a shrink about what's going on inside my head. I have ZERO idea what's going on inside my head and ZERO desire to talk to some stranger. "It'll be a waste of money," I said, which I hoped would work, since their new shop over in Redmond hasn't caught on.

My mom would have let it go, but not my dad. Their sub shops are closed on Mondays, so he spent the morning making phone calls. After dinner he dragged me off to see Dr. Gipson, a skinny, gray-haired guy who has an office by Green Lake, across from the basketball courts. All the

213

other offices in the building were closed, so my dad must have wrangled an emergency appointment.

Once we were alone, I told Dr. Gipson straight up that I didn't want to be there. He said that was fine, but he still asked me a bunch of questions. I mumbled answers, saying things like "I don't know" and "I'm not sure," over and over.

Dr. Gipson finally gave up, called my dad in, and said that I needed more time to process, whatever that means. My dad nodded, and I breathed a sigh of relief. As we were leaving, Dr. Gipson handed me a notebook. "Talking is best," he said, "but until you're ready, putting your thoughts on paper is a good second."

"I'll give it a try," I told him, glad to be getting away.

Back in my room, I tossed the notebook into my bottom drawer, took a shower, tried to play video games. The whole time, though, a thought kept going through my head, something that I need to say to you. It's not much, and it won't change anything, but I want you to know that I'm sorry, that every single cell and molecule and atom inside me is sorry.

Nate

2

MY PARENTS DON'T WANT ME sitting home alone for what's left of spring break, so Tuesday they make me go in with them to the Redmond shop. I'm the dishwasher, and I think I'm going to hate it, but I end up wishing there were more customers, more dishes to wash, more work to keep my mind turned off.

Washing dishes gets me through the week, but on the Sunday night before I go back to Shilshole High, nerves hit. How am I supposed to act? Beaten down and sad? Bucking up and brave?

In the morning, I time my walk so that I reach Shilshole as the first bell sounds. When I sit down in Mr. Filson's math class, Ms. Clyburn's voice comes over the intercom. "As most of you have heard, one of your classmates, Lucas Cawley, died in a drowning accident on the Nooksack River. This is a tragic loss to the school community, and to the larger community as well. Let's observe a moment of silence in his memory."

As Mr. Filson bows his head, the girl next to me mouths,

"Who?" to a friend, who shrugs and mouths back, "No clue." The silence drags on until the principal's voice returns. "Let us keep Lucas in our thoughts and let us all treasure this precious gift of life."

Mr. Filson takes a deep breath and exhales. "You're not invulnerable," he says. "You may think you are, but you're not." More silence before he slides his teacher's manual so that page 203 is visible on the whiteboard behind him. "You can correct your own," he says.

All day I feel as if the building is filled with fog. Faces are hazy; words are muffled. When the final bell sounds, I slip out a side door and head home. All I want to do is go to my room, close my door, and play video games for hours, so when I see Richard and Sara on their knees yanking weeds from the flower beds, my body tenses.

Richard has never done anything to me, or to anyone, as far as I know, but he scares me. The huge motorcycle, the sexy girlfriend, the tattoos. I don't want him asking me questions, wanting me to explain. I stay on my side of the block, never looking his way, and slip quietly into my house.

3

THE WEEDING IS JUST THE start. Tuesday afternoon, a Sky Nursery truck is in front of the Cawley house. Instead of picking up planter boxes from Bill, the driver unloads flats of flowers—marigolds for sure, and other flowers that are light purple and deep red, pink and golden.

It's all explained at dinner. "Richard is having a memorial service for Lucas on Saturday," Mom says as she slides a card toward me.

The invitation gives the date, time, and address. At the bottom, there's a handwritten note:

Nate—
   Tell Lucas's friends from school that they're invited.
   Richard

"You can do that, can't you?" Mom says when I look up. My dad's eyes are on me, too.

"Sure, no problem," I say, but it is a problem.

I never saw Lucas hanging out with anybody. Did my parents expect me to go table to table in the cafeteria asking kids to spend Saturday afternoon at a memorial service for somebody they hardly knew?

Back in my room, I get out my phone, make a group of all the Shilshole High kids in my contact list, and send a text giving the date, time, address—all that stuff. Next, I send the same text to Coach Dawson. It's a sucky way to get the word out, but sucky beats nothing.

By Friday, Richard and Sara have mowed and edged the lawn and filled the flower beds with flowers. The yard isn't garden-magazine beautiful, but it looks good.

Early Saturday morning I watch from my bedroom window as a Handy Andy rental truck unloads about thirty gray folding chairs and two long tables. Richard and Sara set up the chairs in semicircles of six, with the long tables off to the side. At twelve forty-five they bring out trays of food that they place on the tables along with vases of still more flowers. Everything looks great—as if for a graduation or a wedding.

The closer it gets to one o'clock, the sicker I feel. Not a single kid from school has texted me back, not even Hanna, and I haven't heard from Coach Dawson either.

"Let's go, Nate," Dad calls. "It's time."

"Shouldn't we wait?" I say when I'm downstairs. "If we go now, we might be the only ones there."

Mom frowns. "That's why we're going. I'm not having them sitting over there alone."

Ms. Clyburn and Mr. Filson and other teachers from school arrive just as we do. After that, people who live on the block come: the Roths, the Fiorinis, the Nelsons, and others whose last names I don't know. As people enter the yard, they shake hands with Bill and Richard, who are standing by the food table. Bill's eyes are watery; Richard is stone-faced. Megan stands next to Sara, a couple of steps behind Richard. Lucas's mother isn't there, but it would have been strange if she had been.

Coach Dawson shows up. I hear her explain to Bill and Richard that the Champions team is at a tournament in Boise, or many more would have attended, which I don't believe.

The food is good: different kinds of cheese and ham and salami; bread and crackers; Coke, Sprite, and sparkling water. For dessert, there are brownies and cookies. People talk quietly as they eat. I pick up the same words over and over. *Sad* . . . *Terrible* . . . *Hard to believe.* Every few minutes, Sara and Richard collect the used cups and paper plates and take them away.

When Richard sees that people are finishing their food, he flips over one of Bill's flower boxes, steps up on it, and talks for a few minutes about what a good brother Lucas was to Megan and what a help he was to Bill and his mother, and how there is a hole in the family that can never be filled. My mom cries, and so do others. As Richard is finishing, my eyes drift to Megan. That blank look is still there.

After Richard steps down, people stand, shake Bill's hand, and leave. My mom looks at my dad, nods, and I know we're leaving too. I'm turning for home when Richard taps me on the shoulder and motions for me to follow him to a spot away from the others.

I break into a sweat, afraid he'll make me go through Nook-sack again. Instead, he asks if I would help him.

"Sure. Anything," I say.

"Lucas waited with Megan in the morning until her school bus came, right?"

I picture Lucas with his sister. "Always," I say.

"Sara and me are returning to Anacortes tomorrow. Megan will be going back to school on—"

I jump in. "I can wait with her. She knows me and sort of trusts me." I pause. "And after school I could—"

Richard nods toward the shed. "No worries about after school. Bill will be in the shed, working. And this won't be for long. I'm moving them all up to Anacortes as soon as I find a place." He stops and looks around. "Nothing for any of us here."

x x x

Hey Lucas—

I thought that first time would be a one-off, and I know this sounds borderline crazy, but writing to you made you seem less dead, which made me feel less like the walking dead, so I'm back.

I'm guessing you're worried about Megan. I promised Richard that I'd wait with her for her school bus the way you always did, and I want you to know how it worked out.

I was afraid that she'd freak when she saw me and would stay inside, but once I reached the sidewalk in front of your house, your back door swung open and out she came. I said hello, but you know how she is. She moved to a spot ten feet from me and stared at the ground.

When her bus pulled up, she climbed in, found her seat, and put her hands up against the glass the way she always did with you, which blew me away. Maybe she thought I was you, or maybe she wanted me to be you. Anyway, I put my hands up matching hers, and we kept them that way until the bus started off. Then I waved, and she waved back. So if you've been worrying about Megan getting to school okay, don't. I got it.

Nate

4

BO STOPS ME IN THE hallway before school, which startles me. It has been two weeks since Nooksack, and I haven't talked to him or to Colin, and as far as I can tell, they haven't talked to one another.

"You'll probably think I'm a wuss," he says, "but I'm transferring to King's Christian. Today is my last day. My parents blame what happened at Nooksack on Colin, but that's not—" He stops. "Anyway, I can't look at him now and—no offense—I don't much like looking at you, either. You get what I'm saying?"

"Yeah, I get it," I say. "But you'll be missed around here."

He scoffs at that. "Nobody's going to miss me. Colin has talked Charles and Manny into transferring here. One of them will slide into my spot." He pauses. "If I ask you something, will you tell me the truth?"

"Yeah, sure," I say.

He looks off to the side. "My dad says that Colin leads me

around by the nose, that I'm not my own person. He says Colin has been doing it for years, and that's why I've got to get away. Do you think that's true?"

"No," I say, which is a lie.

"I don't think it is either," he says. "You don't know this, but it was my—"

The warning bell rings.

"It was your what?" I ask.

"Nothing," he answers. "Never mind." Then he sticks his hand out, and we shake the way old guys do.

At the end of the day, I see him in the office, turning in his textbooks. For a second, I think about going in and saying goodbye again, but I don't.

x x x

Hey Lucas—

Me again. Something has happened that I hope you'll be okay with. I was eating lunch by myself at a table in the corner of the cafeteria, doing my best to mimic your leave-me-alone vibe, when Colin flopped down into a chair across from me.

"This okay?" he asked.

Once he was settled in, he started to tell me about Bo transferring to King's Christian. I stopped him and told him that I knew. Then he told me that Bo quit Champions, too. "I don't get it," he said. "Things happen in life. You don't hide from them. You man up, right?"

As I nodded my head, he fixed me with those eyes of his and asked when I'd be heading back to Champions.

For the last week, my parents have been asking the same question, so I had an answer ready. "Pretty soon," I said.

He scrunched up his face. "What does that mean?"

"It means pretty soon," I repeated.

He sat back. "Next year is Coach Varner's last year. You've heard that, right?"

"Yeah," I said, "I've heard."

"If the old guy is going to get a Metro title, we're his last chance. We've got to pull together, all of us, and the sooner we start pulling, the better."

I nodded some more.

"So why not come to Champions tomorrow. What's holding you back?"

"Nothing," I admitted.

"So, you'll be there?"

"Yeah," I said, giving in. "I'll be there."

He smiled, gave me a punch on the arm, stood, and went to sit with Hanna.

I know he bullied me some, but I'm okay with going back, and I hope you're okay with it, too. Because what got us to Nooksack? Basketball. That promise we made to one another? That was basketball. I can't put up a plaque for you or visit your grave because I don't know if you were buried or cremated or what. And what good would that do anyway?

What I can do is keep playing, keep improving, finish what we started—or at least try to. When I'm on the court, you're on the court.

Nate

5

WHEN I WENT TO CHAMPIONS with Lucas, I never noticed the bus ride. We got on and—bang—we were there. Without Lucas, the bus crawls down Fifteenth, crawls across the Ballard Bridge, and then crawls some more before it reaches the stop across from Whole Foods.

As I cross Fifteenth, the dogs penned up at the animal shelter start howling. I talk to them the way Lucas and I always did, and as usual it does no good. Nearing the armory gym, I keep waiting for that itchy, ready-to-go feeling to hit me, but it never comes. I stand at the bottom of the stairs for a long time before gathering the courage to climb up and push open the gym doors.

As soon as Colin spots me, he jogs over. We do the knuckle bump, good-to-see-you thing, pretending we're best friends forever. The next knuckle bump comes from Coach Dawson. "Great to have you back, Three," she says. Other guys surround me, including Charles Chenier and Manny Suarez. "Missed you, bro" . . . "Hey, hey" . . . "Good to see you."

This goes on for a minute or two before Coach Dawson blows her whistle. "All right, Champions, back to your warm-ups." As the guys head to the courts, she looks down at my gym bag. "Get changed, Three," she says. "Nobody's waiting on you."

I feel good walking into the locker room. I feel good unzipping my bag, pulling out my shorts and my jersey. This is the right thing to do, like everybody says.

I sit down, start to untie my shoes, and the good feelings drain out of me. From the gym come basketball sounds—shoes squeaking, coaches shouting, whistles blowing. I need to get out there, but I sit.

A knock is followed by Coach Dawson's voice. "You decent in there, Three?"

I swallow and manage: "Yeah."

The door inches open, our eyes catch, and her tough look melts away. She comes to the bench and sits next to me. "What's up?" she asks.

"I don't know," I tell her. "I just—" And then my eyes well up.

"It's okay, Nate," she says softly. "We're all wired differently. You come back when the time is right."

I nod, and then I start crying.

I didn't cry when I saw Lucas's dead body, or with Detective Strauss, or at the memorial, but I bawl my eyes out sitting on the locker room bench with Coach Dawson's arm around me.

She stays until I pull myself together. "I've got to get back or they'll fire my butt," she says, and then she points toward an emergency exit. "No alarm or anything on that door. Quickest way out, and you won't see anyone."

The dogs howl again as I approach the bus stop, but I don't try to talk them down. As the northbound bus comes into view, my guts turn over and I puke into the bushes. I'm still wiping my mouth as the bus door hisses open.

"You been drinking, kid?" the driver asks.

"No," I mumble. "I just don't feel great."

He gives me a hard look. "Get on," he finally says, "but sit up front and holler if you need me to stop. No barfing on my bus."

I look out the window as the bus rumbles along. My parents aren't expecting me until after nine. If I return early and tell them the truth, they'll drag me to see that shrink.

Not happening.

I don't want to roam around for hours, so I take RapidRide past my stop, get off at the McDonald's on Holman Road, and walk to Crown Hill Community Center. Since nobody knows me there, I can hide out.

Inside, I plop down in front of a TV mounted on a wall in the game room. Around me, a handful of elementary and middle school kids are playing Ping-Pong, foosball, Pop-A-Shot, and pool. The sounds of a full-court basketball game leak out from the gym.

I half watch TV for a while. Then, out of nowhere, I find myself thinking about Bill, and how I'm stuck at Nooksack with the water and the canoe and Lucas, the same way he is stuck in Afghanistan.

I'm trying to figure out how to get unstuck when the door to the gym opens and the basketball players—all men in their twenties and thirties—spill out. The first one out is a tatted-up guy who looks like a Hells Angel. "Tammy," he hollers, "we're out of here!" A fifth- or sixth-grade girl who'd been reading in a corner jumps up and races to catch up with him. The other kids who'd been clustered around the Ping-Pong and foosball tables meet up with their fathers and leave.

It's closing time, which means it's time for me to get home.

I'm heading for the door when seeing one guy's sweat-drenched T-shirt sets off alarm bells in my head. I have just enough time to hurry to the men's room, pull out my Champions jersey, splash water under the armpits and down the back. I get my hair wet and mess it up to finish the look.

When I step inside my house fifteen minutes later, my parents are waiting. "Looks like you went at it hard," Mom says.

I tell her I did, and that I'm looking forward to going back.

The second part isn't a lie, because I've decided that I needed that crying jag, but now that it's out of my system, I'll be okay.

6

I **WAKE UP THE NEXT** morning feeling strong. I get dressed, eat some breakfast, see Megan onto the bus, match hands with her, and wave goodbye.

Walking to school, I psych myself to talk to kids in the hallways and in class and at lunch. I *need* to get back to being me. It doesn't happen, though, and I end up doing my Lucas imitation—into one class, sit through the hour, speed walk, head down, eyes forward to my next class.

At lunch, I've taken two bites of my sandwich when Colin comes up. "What's the deal, Nate?" he says, his hands open in front of him.

I shake my head. "It didn't feel right," I say.

He sits down. "Look, I feel terrible about Cawley. Everybody at school feels—"

I hate hearing Lucas's name come out of his mouth. "I'll be there tonight," I say, cutting him off. "I promise. I just needed another day."

He stands. "All right, then. See you there."

x x x

Hey you—

So, here's how my second try at returning to Champions played out. I took the RapidRide to Whole Foods. Totally normal. I got off, and the dogs howled at me. Totally normal. I walked past the animal shelter, past the storage place, turned the corner. All of it just like we used to do.

Then it changed, because the instant I saw the armory gym, a roaring filled my head, and a rush of heat went through my body. I was fifty yards from the gym—a minute away—but I couldn't get myself to take another step. I waited for whatever was happening to stop, but the roaring only grew louder. Finally, I gave up. As soon as I turned my back on Champions, my legs moved like legs again, and I could breathe.

Twenty minutes later I was at Crown Hill Community Center, where I watched a Mariners game on TV, though I couldn't tell you a thing that happened. Before nine I splashed water under the armpits of my jersey. Twenty minutes after that, I was lying to my parents about how great practice was.

Here's the thing, Lucas. I don't know what's wrong with me, so I don't know how to get myself right. But playing for Champions? Wearing the Champions' jersey, going to Champions' practices, running up and down the Champions' court as if Nooksack never happened? That's disrespecting you, and I won't do it.

I'm not quitting hoops. I'm going to keep playing ball for both of us, like I promised. I will never go back on that. I just need to find another way to move forward, to keep improving, and I will.

Nate

7

I KNOW WHAT'S COMING, SO I'm ready. "I'm done with Champions," I say when Colin drops into the chair across from me at lunch.

"Done? Like you're never going back?" he says.

"Exactly like that," I say.

"So you're not playing ball next year?" he asks.

"I'm going to play," I say.

"Really?"

"Yeah," I say. "Really."

He snorts. "You want to know the truth, Dravus? You had a couple of good games. Big frickin' deal. Lots of guys have a couple of good games. If you think you can shoot around in front of your house and then make varsity, you're in la-la land. You need Champions."

"I'll take my chances," I say.

He looks away for a moment. When he looks back, his eyes have gone dark. "Your whole *Look at sad me* act is a scam. You treated Cawley like crap, the same as the rest of us. You know it; I know it; everybody in this school knows it."

He stares me down, waiting for an answer, but I say nothing. Finally he gets up and heads back to his table.

The end.

Or almost the end, because that drama king accusation keeps playing in my head. It doesn't feel true, and I hope it isn't. I don't want to be that person.

✗ ✗ ✗

Hey Lucas—

I've got to ask you something, but before I do, I need to tell you what happened, or my question won't make sense.

Tonight was a Champions night. Since my parents still think I'm practicing with them, after dinner I packed my gym bag and took the bus to Crown Hill, where I half watched TV until it was time to splash water on my jersey and head home. That's what I do every Champions night.

Back inside my home, I talked to my parents a little, took a shower, and climbed into bed. While I was doing all this, a storm had blown in from Puget Sound.

You wouldn't know this, but when it's windy, the shadows cast by the branches of your corkscrew willow glide back and forth on my ceiling. Tonight, though, it was as if the shadows weren't from willow branches, but from basketball players moving up and down a basketball court. I lay in bed watching the shadow game for about twenty minutes, certain I was imagining the whole thing, when I heard a ball being dribbled in the street.

Who'd be playing basketball at midnight during a storm? Nobody. Yet, there it was—thump . . . thump . . . thump—the same sound I used to hear when you'd go out and shoot around under the streetlight late at night.

I dragged myself out of bed, shuffled to my window, pulled back the curtain, and stared down at the street in front of your house. The moon was up, but the sky was cloudy. I could sort of see someone moving under the streetlight, and I could sort of hear a ball being dribbled. It wasn't Richard; he and Sara are up in Anacortes. Megan? That made no sense. Not Bill or your mother. So, here's my question.

Was that you?

Nate

8

IT'S A SCHOOL MORNING, AND it starts like every other. I pour myself a bowl of cereal, peel the top off a container of yogurt, and stick two pieces of bread in the toaster. My dad swallows a mouthful of Grape-Nuts, scratches the side of his face, and says, "How are you feeling, Nate?"

"I'm fine," I say, thinking it's a nothing question, like *Do you think it's going to rain?*

That's when my mom sits down across from me and gives me her deep stare. "What your dad means is, how are you coping?"

"I'm fine," I repeat, but my voice is off.

Mom notices. "That's what people who aren't fine say."

"But I am," I say. "Really."

"We're not seeing friends stopping by," Dad says. "We're not hearing you on your phone. It seems like you're flying solo."

"I've got friends," I say. "I talk to Hanna and Colin at school. There are a couple of Blanchet High kids at Champions, Charles and Manny, who I'm getting tight with. Both might transfer to Shilshole next year, which would be great."

Dad bobs his head. "That's good to hear."

Mom isn't done.

"What happened to Lucas was terrible," she says, "but it was an accident. You know that, right?"

"Right," I say. "I know that."

"So you're not beating yourself up?" Dad says.

"No. I'm doing okay. Really, I am."

They look at each other, some understanding passes between them, and the questions end, at least for a while.

x x x

Hey you—

Me again—who else?

That first time, the shadowy basketball player on the stormy night? I put that down to lack of sleep, but now I'm not sure.

I woke up last night around two a.m., tossed and turned for a while, and ended up staring at the shadows on my ceiling. That's when I heard the *thump-thump-thump* of a basketball, the same as the first time.

I slipped to my window and looked out. There it was— the hoop that Bill had hammered into the willow tree. Above it, the branches moving in the wind, casting the shadows that somehow end up gliding across my ceiling.

I looked closer and thought I saw a person—you—in those shadows. Once I picked you out, I started seeing other people playing in that shadow game, including somebody who looked like me. We're racing up and down the court like NBA stars, feeding off one another. I stared so hard for so long that my eyes went blurry. I blinked a few times, and when I looked back, the hoop, the tree, the shadows were there, but the shadowy players were gone.

Listen.

I know you're dead and nothing can change that. But if your spirit or your soul or some part of you is out there in the night shooting hoops, then keep shooting them. I like thinking that a shadow you is playing, and that a shadow me is on the court with you.

Nate

9

TWO THINGS I WISH WEREN'T true—but are. First, Colin is right. Shooting around in front of my house, pretending I'm going one-on-one against NBA stars, isn't going to cut it. The Shilshole guys who joined Champions—Tony Nevin, Bryce Chambers, Flynn Westwood, and the rest—are all getting coached on fundamentals. They're learning one another's games, becoming a team, preparing for a run at the Metro title. Working out on my own, I can MAYBE keep my skills the same, but staying the same means falling behind.

Second, Colin and Hanna have become an established item, so I can forget about her. They're running as a couple to be copresidents of the school next year. The election is in June, and they'll win easy. Colin hangs all over her in the lunchroom and in the hallways. Even when he's not with her, he walks around campus with a big smile on his face, the happiest guy in the world. Sometimes, though, he'll catch my eye and his grin will disappear for an instant, as if we're back on the banks of the Nooksack. When that happens, he looks away fast.

10

IT'S THE FIRST SATURDAY IN May. When I go downstairs in the morning, Mom is on the phone with Amelia, excitedly talking about a soccer match. League play is in the fall, but Amelia is playing on a club team against top competition. "Two goals!" my mom says. "And Coach Nguyen was at the game."

When it's my turn, Amelia sounds like the Amelia of old. "Something clicked, Nate. I stopped thinking and let myself play. I hope I can keep it going."

"You will," I tell her.

"You know, Nate," she says, "I think I will, too."

I'm happy for her—I really am—but her phone call makes me realize how far I am from where I want to be.

I eat breakfast, lift weights, and then shoot around in the front of the house. After my parents leave for work, I go for a run, ending up at the Ballard Locks. I cross the ship canal to watch the salmon fight their way up the fish ladder from Puget

Sound into Lake Washington. The salmon run is months away, but there are a few early arrivals.

One thing is for sure—salmon aren't quitters. They swim up one step, rest in the calm water for a while, and then take on the next step. If they get swept down to the bottom, they start over.

On my way home, I lean over the railing and watch the water from Lake Washington roar over the spillway back into Puget Sound. It's hypnotizing—the noise, the salty spray, the foam. I get this urge to climb over the rail and jump into the middle of all that wild water. It's a crazy idea. There are workers and tourists all around—one of them would dive in and pull me out. Somebody would call my parents, and my parents would ask a million questions before taking me to Dr. Gipson, who'd ask a million more.

No thanks.

11

I CAN'T FIGURE OUT HOW Lucas took honors classes and held his family together. Okay, Bill helped a little, and maybe his mom did some things, too, but he was the glue. I've got one-tenth of the responsibility he had, but my grades have been in free fall.

They're so bad that my adviser, Ms. Ameera, calls me into her office. She says she knows all about Nooksack, and she puts on a sad face, but then she slides printouts from each of my teachers across the table to me. Highlighted in yellow are my missing assignments.

"I'll do my best from now on," I tell her.

"Forget your best," she says. "Just turn in something. A poor job is better than none."

I'm obsessing over my grades as I walk home, so I don't see Richard and Bill lifting a beat-up sofa onto the bed of a U-Haul pickup truck until I'm almost on top of them.

Lucas was semi-ashamed of Bill, and I would be too if he were my father, but he's a good guy. He saw people being killed, and he can't get that out of his head, so he makes his flower boxes and never hurts anybody.

I cross the street. "You're moving?" I ask.

"Yeah," Bill says as he steps down out of the truck. "We're moving all right. Richard found us a place up in Anacortes near him and Sara."

He gets that long-gone look in his eyes, so I wait. When he comes back, I ask if I can talk to Megan. "To say goodbye," I tell him.

He shakes his head. "Megan and her mom left with Sara a couple of hours ago."

The words are like a punch to my gut. I look at Richard. He gives me a nod, then he and Bill go back into the house for more stuff, and I go into mine. An hour later, the U-Haul truck is gone.

The move is a good thing—I know that. Still, getting Megan onto the bus, matching my hands with hers through the glass, waving to her as the bus pulled away and having her wave back—that was by miles the best part of my day, and now that she's gone, it's gone, too.

12

THE THURSDAY OF MEMORIAL DAY weekend, Amelia comes home.
I hadn't seen her since Nooksack, and the first thing she does is
hug me, which chokes me up. It's a Champions night, so after
dinner, I pretend to head off to practice but as usual take the bus
to Crown Hill.

Sitting in front of the TV, I knock off two math assignments.
When I can't solve a problem, I follow Ms. Ameera's advice, slap
some numbers down, and move on. Before heading home, I hit
the men's room to splash water under the armpits of my jersey
and mess up my hair.

Another night, like the others.

Only it isn't, because when I step into the house, my parents
glare at me. In the kitchen, almost hiding, is Amelia. "Where
were you?" my mom snaps.

"Champions," I say. "Practice."

My mom looks toward Amelia.

"I went to the gym to watch," she says, "but you weren't there. Your coach told me you haven't been there since—"

My dad interrupts. "How about telling us where you have been?"

I come clean about Crown Hill Community Center and get the lecture.

"Disappointed . . . Hurting yourself . . . Trust is everything . . ."

Bottom line is that I've got to get a summer job to repay the money they'd laid out for Champions, and that I can't get my driver's license until January. Neither is a big deal. Wasting their money never felt right, and what do I need a driver's license for? They bring up Dr. Gipson, but after I tell them it'd be another waste, they drop it. "We've thrown away enough money already," my dad says.

Up in my room, I sprawl out on my bed. After a few minutes I hear a tapping on my door.

Amelia.

"You mad at me?" she asks.

"No," I say, even though I am. "They'd have found out eventually."

She sits at the foot of my bed. "Why the lying, Nate? That's not you."

I shrug. "I was afraid that if they found out I'd quit Champions, they'd make me see that shrink."

"Would that be so bad?" she says. "A psychiatrist could help you."

"I don't need help," I say.

She raises her eyebrows. "If you say so." Silence, and then, "Look, I've got things going with friends except for Monday afternoon. Rematch?"

"You got it," I say.

I hardly see her Friday, Saturday, or Sunday. I expect her to cancel the miniature golf, but she doesn't. At first we're playing for fun, but somewhere in there I get serious, which makes her get serious. I haven't competed in anything for a long time, and I miss it. On the last hole I have a six-foot putt to win. When the ball drops into the cup, I feel a rush.

I don't go along when my parents drive Amelia to Sea-Tac after dinner, but before she leaves, she hugs me again. "Love you, Bro," she says as she lets go.

It's after midnight. There's school tomorrow, so I should be sleeping, but I'm wide-awake. Lucas's corkscrew willow has leafed out, and I'm watching a shadow game play out on my ceiling. The players are racing up and down the court, knocking down three-pointers, and rattling the backboard with slam dunks. I'm not stupid—I know there's a ninety-nine percent chance all this is in my head, but so what?

No harm, no foul.

x x x

Hey you—

I haven't written in a while because nothing much has happened, but tonight I caught a break.

I still go to Crown Hill Community Center after dinner. I told my parents that I get more homework done there than anywhere else, which is true, so they're okay with it.

I was finishing up a math assignment when the gym door flew open and a guy around thirty stormed out, holding a bloody towel to his nose and moaning.

Ten seconds later two other guys came out. "You okay, mate?" the one holding a basketball asked over and over.

The nose guy shook his head. "It's broken," he said. Then he pointed at the other guy—a big man wearing a T that read Sports Director—and said, "You broke it, Kekino."

The nose guy flopped down into the chair across from me. I watched him put the towel to his face, then pull it away to look at his blood, then put it back. After a couple of peeks, he stood, picked up his duffel bag, kicked open the exit door, and was gone.

The smaller guy looked at me and motioned with his head toward the gym. "You ball? We're down a player."

The sports director—Kekino—shook his head. "He's a kid, Trey. He can't play."

The guy who'd asked me—Trey—scanned the room. "You see anybody else around here, mate?" he said in what I figure is an Australian accent, because they're the ones who call everybody "mate."

After a little while, Kekino shrugged.

Trey gave me a fist bump and asked my name.

"Lucas," I said.

I know you're thinking—WHAT!!!???

The instant your name came out of my mouth, I was thinking the same thing, but there was no taking it back.

"I'm Gregory," he said as he put his fist out for me to bump, "but the guys call me Trey because I've got the three-point magic in these fingertips." He wiggled them fast, made a shooting motion, and said, "Swish!"

Maybe because I told him I was you, I played like you. I didn't look to score; instead, I did the dirty work—diving for loose balls, setting solid screens, hustling back on D, never quitting on a play. It felt great to sweat, to run, to hear my shoes squeaking on the gym floor, even if it was for only fifteen minutes and even though I didn't score a point.

Nate

13

I **ALWAYS GET TO CROWN** Hill early. If Trey is there—and he usually is—he coaches me up. It turns out he played point guard for Seattle Pacific University. He's built like Steph Curry, and he looks like him too, only Trey has dreads. He's in grad school now, studying to become a PE teacher and eventually a coach.

I'm right about Australia. Most of the time I understand him fine, but not always. One time he asked me what I did to die. I was . . . Huh? Turns out he was asking what I did today.

He tells me to play defense like a Tasmanian devil. I remember hearing about them, but I thought they were made-up creatures, like dragons. It turns out that Tasmanian devils are nasty animals with teeth so sharp they bite through bones. I asked Trey if he'd ever been to Tasmania, and he said, "Nah, I'm from Sydney. Tasmania is the Woop Woop," which is what Australians call the sticks.

The games are for men—no high school students—which

is why Kekino didn't want me playing that first time. He still doesn't like it, but he lets it go.

There are always at least ten men, so I'm never on the court at the start. After the teams get picked, Trey points me out. "If you're winded or you have to leave early," he says to them, "have Lucas take your place." I'm so used to being called Lucas that I don't flinch.

Mainly, I sit in a chair along the sideline, doing my homework, but most nights I get on the court for ten or fifteen minutes. My game—especially my defense—is improving. Craig, the biker guy who screamed at his daughter, snarls at me whenever we're matched up. "Guard somebody else," he said last time.

"You're in his head," Trey says. "That's good. Stay on him."

14

THIS SUMMER I NEED TO play a ton of basketball and get a job to repay my parents the Champions money. That's it. Two things. It should be no big deal, but it's the last day of school and I still haven't come up with a way to do both.

My parents want me to work at one of the sub shops. Amelia did that one summer, and she said the other workers treated her like a spy. I'd man up and take the job, but I'd have to go in with my parents around nine a.m., leaving me with no time to work out in the morning. Lots of days—especially in the summer, with workers taking their vacations—my parents don't make it home until eight or nine at night, which means I wouldn't get home until eight or nine. I could forget about Crown Hill and Trey and any chance of making the varsity team.

I'm eating in the cafeteria, my brain going round and round in search of a solution, when there's a commotion across the room. I look up—it's Colin and Hanna. They won the election—no surprise—and somebody has brought a huge sheet cake into the cafeteria for a celebration. Kids crowd around as they laugh and kiss and shove cake into one another's mouths, acting like newlyweds. I can't watch, so I gather up my lunch and head outside to eat on the stairs. As I'm leaving, Colin's eyes catch mine, and as always, that grin disappears.

As I'm walking through the main lobby, a bunch of seniors are razzing James Vikram, a brainy kid with a long ponytail who wins all the Math Olympiads. "Your career awaits, Vikram," one kid says, pointing to a flyer posted on the bulletin board. "Call Stanford and tell them you don't need their trash scholarship." They laugh and walk away, but I pull the flyer down and shove it in my back pocket.

The job is at Shoreline Golf Club, which is on the 28 bus line. They need somebody to walk the fairways every morning repairing divots. As soon as I get home, I fill out an online application. Within ten minutes, my phone rings and I have the job.

When I tell my parents, their faces tighten. "You sure you'll be okay alone all day?" my dad says. "You know how it is in the summer. Lots of nights we won't make it home until late. Won't it be kind of lonely with Amelia gone?"

I was expecting that, and I've got my answer ready.

I tell them that I'll be working in the morning. Afternoons and nights I'll hang out with friends—swim at Green Lake or go down to Golden Gardens to play beach volleyball. If nobody is around, there's always open gym at the community centers, where I can play pickup basketball. I make it seem as if I'll be busy every second of every day.

It takes a while, but they give in. "Okay, but you text us when you get home from the golf course," Mom says. "And when you go out, text again and tell us where you're going and when you'll be back. Understood?"

They never did all this checking and double-checking on Amelia, but I let it go. "Understood," I say.

I breathe easy for the first time in a long time. Mornings will be a waste, but I'll have afternoons to improve my shot, build my strength, and increase my stamina. Then, at Crown Hill, I'll get game experience against grown men. When varsity try-outs roll around, I'll be the Stealth Bomber. Nobody will see me coming until I'm right there.

x x x

Hey—

I need to tell somebody about tonight's game, so here goes.

Ten guys showed up, but one guy on Trey's team tweaked his knee in the first minute and left, which meant I played the rest of the game. And what a game! The momentum went back and forth with lead changes, great shots, blocks, assists. I was in the zone, and so was everybody else.

We were down one with time running out. From the top of the key, I spotted Trey cutting hard down the lane. I fed him a bounce pass, which he took to the hoop. As the ball slipped through the net, giving us the lead, Frank, the guy from the main desk, poked his head in and shouted, "Last shot!"

As his words echoed through the gym, everybody stopped—everybody except Kekino. He took the inbound pass and was off like a locomotive, rumbling toward the basket. For a big guy, he can motor.

I was the only player with a chance to cut him off. As K thundered downcourt, I judged the angle and slid into position one step inside the free throw line. My instincts were screaming GET OUT OF THE WAY! but I willed my body to stay still and take the charge.

Kekino tried to avoid me, but he's too big to make quick moves. His forearm caught me flush in the chest, sending me sprawling to the floor. He lost his balance and threw up a shot that barely grazed the rim.

"That's it!" the desk guy called out as he turned off the main gym lights.

K reached down to pull me to my feet. "You okay, kid?" he asked. "You hit your head?"

"I'm fine," I gasped. "You just knocked the wind out of me."

By then Trey had reached us. "You got a pair, Lucas," he said. "No brains, but a pair." He high-fived me as the other guys on the team crowded around, slapping me on the back and saying, "Great play, Lucas!" and "Way to hang in there!"

Here's what I want you to know. Trey taught me how to take the proper angle to cut off fast breaks, but the guts to do it? I was channeling you. Lucas Cawley made that play.

Nate

15

BEFORE, WHEN BASEBALL PLAYERS COMPLAINED about the dog days of summer, I never knew what they meant. Now I do because I'm living them.

Every morning, my parents give me a ride to the golf course, which is both good and bad. Good, because not having to take the bus means that I can sleep in. Bad, because for twenty minutes in the car they pound me with questions. "What did you do yesterday?" "You seeing much of Colin?" "How about Hanna?" "Got plans for this afternoon?" They try to sound casual, but they're checking on me.

The divot job is boring, and sometimes worse. One day, I'm hiding behind a bush, holding a bucket filled with a mixture of sand, dirt, and grass seeds, when a guy hits a screaming line drive right at me. The ball whistles through the leaves, coming within six inches of braining me even though I'm fifty yards from where he's aiming. He tromps over and says, "Hey, kid, you see where my ball ended up?" When I shake my head, he glares at me and says, "Next time keep your eyes open." If he'd killed me, he would have stepped over my body and gone on looking for his stupid golf ball.

Once I finish work, I hustle to catch the 28. After I eat lunch, I should get right to my workout, which is what I did the first weeks of summer. Somewhere around the Fourth of July, though, the workouts turned into a grind. Not the shooting parts—I can shoot around in front of the house for hours. The weight lifting is okay, too. But stretching along with that rubber band woman? Running four miles? Jumping a zillion times to gain an inch or two in my vertical leap? Those things get old.

I'm not liking Crown Hill that much, either. Every night, I count the men as they drift in. Sometimes there are just nine, and I'm pumped to play. Then, seconds before the game starts, another guy wanders in, turning me into a spectator. I almost wish I had homework to kill the time. Trey promises that soon guys will quit or go on vacation, and I'll be playing full-time, but it hasn't happened yet.

The shadows from Lucas's willow are still floating across my ceiling, but lately I'm just seeing shadows. I got no game any-where.

16

I THINK I'M ON MY way to full-blown crazy. I write letters to a dead person. I see phantom basketball games on my ceiling. I tell the men at Crown Hill that my name is Lucas. And now I've invented a girlfriend.

Her name is Carlotta, and she works the morning shift at the golf course restaurant. She lives on Crown Hill right by the community center, which is where we hang out. She's got curly brown hair, brown eyes, a round face, and a great smile. She plays volleyball and wishes she was taller so she could spike. She has two younger brothers, Pedro and Alex. Pedro is a top student and a straight arrow, but she worries about Alex. She looks after her brothers every afternoon, and I give her a hand by playing foosball with them, kicking a soccer ball around, playing Ping-Pong—all the regular stuff.

I made up Carlotta because I hate pretending that I'm having a great summer with Colin and Hanna and the rest of their Shilshole crowd. The words just don't want to come out of my mouth. It's a million times easier to invent things around Carlotta and her brothers.

When my parents are home and I'm home—which doesn't happen much—I pretend to talk on the phone with Carlotta. I laugh and say things like "No way! That can't be true." I fake getting texts from her, too. I'll jump up at breakfast, go out of the room for a minute, look at my phone, tap a message to myself, press cancel, and then come back in. "That was Carlotta," I'll say. "After work, we're going to hike down to the beach at Carkeek Park."

I don't like lying to my parents, and I'd stop if they'd back off their daily interrogation, but I don't see that happening anytime soon, which means Carlotta will be a big part of my life for the rest of the summer.

x x x

Hey Lucas—

For the last week, they've been short a player at Crown Hill every night, so I'm on the court full-time.

FINALLY!

Trey works it so that I'm on his team. I told you he wants to be a coach, so he's sacrificing his game to build mine. During warm-ups and at every water break he goes over situations, explaining how to read and react to defenses.

Remember how Coach Dawson would always say, "Move without the ball"? Okay . . . great. But move where? Maybe you knew, but I didn't.

Trey's teaching me when to slash to the hoop, when to spot up for a corner three, and when to just stay out of the way. In the beginning he signaled with his eyes or a small movement of the head. Lately I've been making the right read on my own. If I score, the men pump me up with "Good move, Lucas!" and "Way to cut!" even when they're on the other team. The only player who doesn't is biker-guy Craig. When I score on him, he gets so mad his head looks like it's going to explode. It's comical, but nobody laughs. Whenever I see his daughter out in the game room, I feel for her.

Now that I'm playing full-time, I'm back to pushing myself hard in my afternoon workouts. August is a few days away, which means that before tryouts, I'll have three full months of playing at Crown Hill every night. Colin and the rest of the Champions guys practice only three times a week. Even if you add in their tournaments, I'm still outworking them.

Those goals we set? One week ago, I was thinking: NOT HAPPENING, but I've got a totally different mindset now.

Nate

17

AFTER MEETING WITH MS. AMEERA, I made sure that for every missing assignment, I turned in something, no matter how weak, and some of it was pathetic. I don't think the teachers looked at half of those papers, because most came back with a check mark on top and nothing else. I figured the check marks were Cs, so when my grades come in the mail today, I'm expecting a report card full of Cs. I do a double take when I see nothing but Bs.

My parents come home late, but they've been worrying about my report card, so I bring it downstairs. They stare at the page for a while, nodding their heads.

My dad looks up. "This is really impressive, Nate, especially after what—" He stops and shakes his head, then looks to my mom.

"We are very, very proud of you," she says, "and you should be proud of yourself."

I start to beat it back to my room when my dad asks me to sit for a moment, so I sit.

"We know we haven't been around much this summer," he says, "and unfortunately, we're going to be around even less in August. The Redmond shop is struggling, but you know that, right?"

"I know," I say, picturing them poring over spreadsheets on the kitchen table.

"It's temporary," he says. "In the fall, when vacations end and more Microsoft workers return to the office, things will improve. We'll be real parents again."

"No worries," I say. "I don't feel neglected or anything."

For the second time, I try to escape, and for the second time, I don't make it. "Sit for a minute longer," Mom says. "Your dad has had his say, now I'm going to have mine. I promise it won't take long."

As I sit down, her eyes well up. "This will embarrass you," she says, her voice thick, "but I don't care. A lot of kids your age, left on their own all summer like you've been, they'd have—well let's just say they wouldn't be spending their days helping a friend look after her younger brothers. You know we love you, but I don't think we tell you often enough how much we admire and respect you." As she speaks, my dad is nodding his head.

I feel my face go red as a wave of guilt washes over me. For an insane moment I want to tell them the truth about Carlotta, but the truth would cause trouble.

When I stand, my mom kisses me on the cheek and my dad gives me a hug before I finally make it upstairs to my room.

18

I REMEMBER SEEING A SURFING movie where a guy catches a wave and then rides it for what seems like forever. That's how August goes for me. The job is the job, and I don't let it bother me. In the afternoons, I work out like a possessed man. Sometimes I think I can *feel* myself getting bigger, faster, and stronger every second, as if I have some sort of superpower.

Trey has been working with me on my drives to the hoop. The key, he says, is to absorb the contact, regain your balance, and then finish. Before, I'd shoot as the guy was hitting me. The difference is about a tenth of a second, but since I've started doing it Trey's way, more of my shots are finding the bottom of the net.

Tonight, warming up, he starts quizzing me. What high school do I go to? What's my team like? How's the coach?

"They were one game out of the playoffs last year," I tell

him. "Two guys from Bishop Blanchet are transferring in, so this year they just might take it all, which would be great because the coach is retiring, and he's never won a Metro title."

"Why do you keep saying *they*?" Trey asks. "You're on the team, right?"

I shrug. "I played JV last year," I say. "This summer, lots of the guys are playing for Champions, an AAU team. They'll be way ahead of me. I'll try out, but—"

He motions with his head toward the court. "Mate, you're holding your own every night against men. That's better preparation than AAU ball." Then he smiles. "Besides, you got me coaching you, and I'm the best. You're a lock to make the team."

x x x

Hey you—

School starts soon, which got me thinking about Megan. I've been so focused on basketball that I haven't thought about her for a while, and I'm sorry.

Anacortes is much smaller than Seattle, so I was worrying that they might not have the right kind of school for her. I asked my mom tonight, and she said that every school district has a program for kids like Megan, and that they'll take good care of her. I'm telling you so you won't worry.

I hope Bill is pounding together his planter boxes, and

that your mom has got a hospital job and isn't drinking as much, and that Richard and Sara stop by a lot to do things with Megan. I can picture your whole family, including you, even though I'll never see any of you again.

Nate

19

AMELIA COMES HOME FOR LABOR Day weekend. Her first night back, we eat at Monkey Bridge. All through dinner she talks about how glad she is that she stuck it out at Berkeley; her classes are great, and her team is one big family. She's my sister, so I'm happy for her, but listening to her gets annoying.

I don't see her much after that because she is out with her friends, but tonight she asks me to go with her to see the new Marvel movie at the Majestic Bay. The movies she goes to are indies or old black-and-white films, so she's being nice, but I'm on such a roll at Crown Hill that I don't want to miss a single game.

"I can't," I say, trying to think fast. "I'm playing foosball with Flynn Westwood and some other guys."

My mom shoots me a look. "Nate, your sister is leaving tomorrow, and you won't see her for months. You can play foosball with Flynn Westwood any night. And since when have you been friends with him anyway? Flynn Westwood?"

"Forget it," Amelia says, and she turns, climbs the stairs to her room, and closes her door . . . hard.

"Nice," my dad says. "Well done."

I feel like a cockroach, so I traipse upstairs and knock on her door.

"What?" she snaps.

I step inside and explain about Crown Hill hoops and Trey. When I finish, she rolls her eyes. "Last time I visited," she says, "you were pretending to be playing when you weren't. Now you're pretending not to be playing when you are. Why not tell Mom and Dad the truth?"

"Because it's men's basketball. They'll worry that I don't have friends my own age," I say.

"Do you?" she asks.

"Sure, I do," I say. "I've got lots of friends."

She looks me straight in the eye, and I look straight back at her.

"Okay, here's what we'll do," she finally says. "We'll tell Mom and Dad that I'm going to play foosball with you and Flynn—whoever he is—but instead I'll watch your game. I've wanted to see you play for a long time."

Total panic. I can't say no, but she is sure to hear somebody call me Lucas. How am I going to explain that?

I come up with nothing, so I'm in a state of dread when I push open the door to the Crown Hill gym and head over toward Trey. He smiles and says, "Good to see you, mate," but his eyes are on Amelia, which makes sense. She's an athlete, and she's not bad looking.

I introduce her and then slip away, which suits both of them.

Trey spends the time before the game helping Amelia with her shot, reaching around her shoulder to demonstrate where in her fingertips the ball needs to be. Sometimes they are almost cheek to cheek. I'm too far away to hear what they're saying, but they aren't talking about me.

When it's game-time, I get unbelievably lucky. Amelia sticks in her earbuds and finds a chair, and her head starts bobbing to her tunes. Seconds later, Trey says, "I've got Lucas."

With Amelia watching, I see the court better, jump higher, and run faster. I'm not the star—that's always Trey—but I'm dishing out assists, hauling down rebounds, and knocking down my share of shots. We need it all because Kekino is having his best game in weeks.

The game is tied when Frank comes in and gives his "Last shot" holler. Kekino posts up on the right side, takes an entry pass, and starts backing his guy down. I'm guarding biker-guy Craig, who is camped at the top of the key. I keep waiting for him to slash to the hoop, but he stays stuck—too tired to move. I think, *Okay, take a chance.*

When Kekino looks over his shoulder, I flash into the key, strip the ball from him, and snag it just before it trickles out-of-bounds. Trey has released downcourt; I hit him with a baseball pass, and he goes in for the winning layup. I catch Amelia's eye, and she gives me a huge smile and two thumbs-up.

I do not stick around for the usual "good game" stuff because I'm terrified that she'll take her earbuds out and hear somebody call me Lucas. I don't breathe until we're out the door.

She suggests we go to Frankie and Jo's, a place on Seventieth that sells ice cream made with cashew oil. I expect the stuff to taste awful, but my mocha is great. She orders something called ginger chai, which she has me taste. I tell her it's delicious, but it's terrible.

As we eat the ice cream or the ice cashew, or whatever you call it, she pumps me with questions. How much do I weigh? How much can I bench press? What is my vertical leap? When I tell her I don't know my height, she says that I've had a growth spurt and am at least six foot three. "You're going to play a lot this year," she says. "Trust me. A lot."

An hour later, when I turn out the light and climb into bed, I'm in a glow. So many things could have gone wrong, and nothing did. I rest my head on my pillow, look at the shadows dancing back and forth on my ceiling, and settle in for a great game, with me and Lucas making steals, driving the lane for layups, knocking down threes, hounding the other team into turnovers.

We're going to win big tonight; I can feel it.

20

TOTALLY—AND I MEAN TOTALLY—SUCKY DAY. First sucky thing is being back at Shilshole High, which is way worse than I thought it would be. Last April, after Nooksack, there weren't that many days until school ended, so I knew I could survive. This year—staring at ten months with my head down, eating lunch alone, no friends, no nothing—it's grim.

The one class I think might be okay is PE, but even that turns out to be a fail. The class has sixty guys and two teachers, Coach Varner and Coach Schmidt. When I see Coach Varner's name on my schedule and I see Colin in the locker room, I fantasize about taking Colin to the cleaners in one-on-one games, with Varner watching my every move.

So what happens?

The first thing Varner and Schmidt do is divide us into two groups of thirty. Colin goes with Varner. I go with Schmidt. End of any chance to show Varner how much game I've got.

Sucky thing number two happens at dinner. Out of nowhere,

my parents start grilling me about my plans after high school. Did I want to go to college? Did I want to learn a trade? Did I want to someday manage one of their shops?

I'm clueless about my future, other than knowing I don't want to work for them. I say that I'm thinking about a job at a hospital. I have no idea where that came from, but my mom pounces on it, telling me she's certain that Bellevue College has certificate programs for medical sonography technicians and other jobs I've never heard of. "You'll make a good salary," she says, "while doing a good thing."

After dinner, I beat it out of there, saying I'm going to Crown Hill Community Center to do homework. I know they think I'm also meeting Carlotta, and I let them think it.

Once I step inside the gym, the suckiest thing of all smacks me in the face. Instead of seeing the regular eight or nine men, there are at least fourteen. Men who I thought had quit have come back, and there are some new faces too. I catch Trey's eye, and he motions me to a corner, where he tells me that it's the first night of the fall class.

"Men's basketball," he says. "It's the same setup as before, but a new session. First few days, everybody comes, but after that, not so much. You'll be playing again real soon, but not tonight, mate."

He coaches me on a side hoop for fifteen minutes, but once the five-on-five game starts, I drag myself to the TV room to watch a replay of Sunday's Seahawks–Rams game. As I'm watching, I hear the muffled sounds of the basketball game and the louder squeals of the kids hanging out in the game room.

When I get home, my parents are hunched over the kitchen table working numbers on their shops. I go upstairs, play some *Mortal Kombat*, and watch a shadow game, which is the only game I'll have for a while.

21

A WILD NIGHT AT CROWN Hill, and I'm still shaking.

When I push open the door to the gym, I do a quick count, like I've done for the last three weeks. Just six players, so right away I'm thinking this could be the night when I'm back to playing full-time. As Trey and I warm up on a side hoop, I keep one eye on the door. Player number seven shows up six minutes before game-time. Player eight arrives two minutes later. The adrenaline is going—I'm willing that door to stay closed. Three minutes. Two minutes. One minute. Right as Kekino blows his whistle to start the session, the door opens and biker-guy Craig walks in, alone. He's player nine, making me player ten.

Trey gives me a knuckle bump. "I told you," he says.

We choose up sides, Trey making sure I'm on his team. As usual, biker-guy Craig is on Kekino's. When Trey tells me to guard Craig, Craig scowls. "I am so sick of you," he says, and Trey shoots me a smile.

The game starts slowly—ten minutes of everybody playing

nicey-nice. Then, as Craig is going up for a rebound, he throws a wild elbow that catches me on the side of the head and knocks me to the ground. I'm dazed for a few seconds, but when I look up, Trey—his face contorted by rage—is trying to get at Craig. Kekino has him wrapped up in a bear hug.

As I get to my feet, Craig screams, "Let him go, K! If he wants a piece of me, he's got it!"

Kekino wraps Trey tighter and uses his size to push Trey clear across the gym to the far side of the court. Other guys step in front of Craig, making sure he stays where he is. Nothing happens for a while, but once Trey has calmed down, Kekino releases him, goes back across center court, and gets in Craig's face.

"This is a friendly game," he says. "Keep your elbows in."

Craig snorts. "I barely touched the kid," he says. "It's not my fault if he's a snowflake."

Kekino moves even closer so that they're nose-to-nose. "You can keep your elbows in," he says, "or you can leave the gym. Your choice."

Silence for a long moment, then Craig shrugs. "Let's just play."

It's over, but it isn't. Both teams huddle for a moment to get refocused.

"I'll guard Craig," Trey says.

I shake my head. "No, no. I got him." Trey doesn't argue; he knows I can't back down.

The game starts up again. First possession, Craig posts me up. One of their guards feeds him the ball, and he slowly backs me down. I bump him, trying to keep him from his spot, but he's stronger. He turns, rises, and banks home an eight-footer.

Trey knows I want the ball. He crosses the center line, passes to me on the wing, and then motions for everybody else to clear out, leaving me one-on-one with Craig. I crouch and swing the ball back and forth in front of me, as if I'm preparing to drive to the hoop. Craig is afraid I'll blow by him, so he backs off two steps, giving me a clean look. Take what they give you—that's smart basketball—so that's what I do, draining a twenty-footer.

We're even.

The tension between us is contagious. There are shoves in the back on rebounds, hard bumps on drives to the hoop, a hand in the face on every jump shot. The game is so rough that neither team gets into any kind of flow—an ugly game, but a close one.

The score is tied when we hear the familiar "last shot" ring out across the gym. Kekino holds up his hand, and the game stops. "Frank," he says, "how about leaving the lights on until the next made basket? This game needs a winner."

Frank groans. "Make it quick. I don't get overtime pay." Kekino looks at Trey, and Trey nods, signaling we're ready.

Their guard brings the ball into the forecourt. The smart play would be to have Kekino take the shot, but Craig has posted me up and is waving for the ball—and he gets it. He starts backing me down the same as before, but we've been playing for an hour, and he's tired. He stops a couple of feet from where he wants to be, gathers himself, and goes up for the shot. But he barely goes up at all—his legs are dead—and I block his shot. The ball bounces toward the corner, where Trey recovers it.

There's no chance for a fast break, so Trey slowly dribbles the ball across midcourt. I figure he'll take our shot, but instead he fires a pass to me on the wing and then motions for the other guys to clear out.

This is it.

Craig is up close on me, anticipating that I'll try to shoot over him. I'm watching his eyes, and when I see him lose focus, I take a hard dribble to the right and then cross over on him. He tries to stay with me, but his feet get tangled and he falls on his butt. I kiss the ball off the backboard, it goes down and through, and the game is ours.

When Craig gets up, he gives me a death stare and then stomps out. Once he's gone, Trey breaks into a huge grin, which I match.

I'm still flying high when I get home. From the front room, I hear my dad's voice. "Come out here, Nate," he says. "You've got to see this."

My mom's iPad is set up on the coffee table. The Cal women are tied with Stanford, with a couple minutes left. My parents are sitting on the edge of the sofa, holding hands, eyes excited. I don't get it, and then I do. With time running out, Amelia makes a steal, races down the sideline, controlling the ball as she angles toward the Stanford goal. Fifteen yards out, she stops on a dime, losing her defender, and blasts a rocket into the upper-right corner, the winning goal. Her teammates swarm her, knocking her down in a lovefest.

"Cal–Stanford is like Washington–Oregon," my mom says, beaming. "They'll be talking about Amelia's goal for years."

"That's great," I say. "Good for her."

I want to tell them about my game, but they think I'm doing homework with Carlotta and then playing Ping-Pong and foosball with her brothers, so I keep my mouth shut.

✕ ✕ ✕

Hey you—

This is the week PE teachers administer the school district's physical fitness tests. You remember them—some sprints, some middle-distance races, a quickness test, standing jump, long jump, push-ups, sit-ups, pull-ups.

I've always loafed through them—who really cares? But this year I worked it so that I ended up in the same group as Colin.

When he saw me next to him, he didn't say a word, but he knew that it was on. We both went full-out in every event. I beat him in the shuttle run by two-tenths of a second, and I beat him again in the 440 by five yards. Okay—I admit it—he took me in everything else, but he didn't crush me like he used to. I'm not just feeling bigger, faster, and stronger—I am bigger, faster, and stronger. No doubt about it.

Nate

22

BIKER-GUY CRAIG HADN'T BEEN AT Crown Hill for two weeks, and he wasn't there tonight when the game started. I was hoping I'd never see him again, but no luck with that.

We'd been going for about ten minutes when he walked in. You come late, everybody knows you've got to wait your turn. Even Trey and Kekino would wait if they were late.

Craig is standing behind one of the hoops, a sour look on his face, when the ball gets knocked out-of-bounds. He scoops it up, points at me, and says, "Off the court, kid. I'm taking your spot."

Trey jumps in. "Hold on, mate," he says. "Your chance will come."

Craig ignores Trey, looks to Kekino, and again points at me. "Is this kid registered?"

"What?" K says.

"You heard me," he says. "Is he registered for the class?"

"Come on, Craig," K answers, "you don't want to do this."

"Yeah, I do," Craig says. "If he's not in the class, I want him off the court and out of the gym. Permanently."

"He's no problem," K says, holding his hands out, palms up.

"No problem?" Craig scoffs. "Say one of us knocks him down and he breaks his neck. The kid's parents sue. What are you going to say, Kekino? That you knew he was too young, but you let him play? That we all knew, and we all let him play? How do you think that'll fly in court?"

"I'm not going to get hurt," I say. "And my parents wouldn't sue if I did."

Craig ignores me, pulls out his phone. "You want me to call the head of the Parks Department?" he says. "See what he thinks about one of his employees letting an underage kid play in a men's game?"

K takes a deep breath, exhales, thinks for a while, and then turns to me. "Lucas, you're going to have to go," he says.

"That's not—" I start.

"The man is right," Kekino says. "You should be playing with guys your own age."

I wait for Trey to say something, but there's silence. I pick up my gym bag and walk out into the lobby, and I'm about to leave for good when Trey's voice stops me. "Hey, Lucas," he says. "Sorry."

"That guy is such a jerk," I say.

"Yeah," Trey says, "but your school season is a couple of weeks away. Once that starts, you'd have no time to come here."

He reaches a fist toward me; I give it a bump.

As I'm walking away, he calls out, "You go to Shilshole High, right?"

"Yeah," I say. "Why?"

"You never know," he says. "I might just show up at one of your games."

I spend the first half of the walk home feeling miserable before admitting to myself that getting kicked out isn't all bad. I can stop all the lies about Carlotta, which have been wearing me down. I'll tell my parents that she's so busy with volleyball that she isn't going to Crown Hill anymore, so I'll be studying at home. They'll probably feel sorry for me, thinking she dumped me, but there's nothing I can do about that.

x x x

Hey you—

Tonight was Halloween. I told my parents I was going with some of the guys on last year's JV team to a haunted house at Piper Village in Greenwood.

I left the house around seven and headed down to the Ballard Locks to watch the salmon. On my way, I passed your house. Your porch light was on; your walkway was lined with smiling pumpkins; paper lanterns dangled from the eaves.

You wouldn't know this, but when you lived there, your house was scarier than the houses with witches and skeletons and creepy music. No lights on inside or out. Curtains pulled tight. Not a sign of life. What was up with that? Were you all just sitting there in the dark?

I hope it's different now that your family is in Anacortes. I have this scene playing out in my head where Richard and Sara buy Megan a costume and walk with her as she trick-or-treats with friends from her school. She doesn't have lots of friends, and she doesn't get lots of candy, but she's happy.

Nate

23

WHEN I JOIN THE LINE in the office to turn in my basketball forms, Charles—who's in front of me—tells me he didn't think I'd try out. "Because of your friend Lucas," he says. "Once you quit Champions, I figured you were done with basketball."

"I've been playing in a men's league up in Crown Hill," I say. "It's been good."

The line moves forward, and we're both quiet for a while. "I got to tell you," he says. "The whole thing with Lucas seems off."

"How?" I ask.

"First of all," he says, "nobody mentions him. I said something to Colin about him, and he just shook his head. Same with Tony Nevin, with everybody. At Bishop Blanchet, a basketball player died ten years ago in a car crash and his picture is still up in the trophy case. Lucas Cawley hasn't been dead a year and he gets nothing?"

What could I say? That Lucas Cawley wasn't his name at all. That he was Creepy Crawley, that kids laughed at him when he was alive, which is why no one wants to think about him now that he's dead?

The secretary calls out "Next," and Charles steps forward. She goes over his papers, and then it's my turn, and by the time she finishes with me, Charles is gone.

That conversation has me off stride, and then, at lunch, Hanna comes over to my corner spot in the cafeteria, sits down across from me, and asks how I'm doing. I haven't talked to her in weeks, and my hands go all clammy as I give her my—"Everything's great. No problems at all"—answer.

She nods and puts her hand on top of mine, and I'm totally embarrassed about the sweat, which I know she can feel. "I care about you, Nate," she says. "You know that, don't you?"

"Yeah," I say, my face reddening. "I know."

"So when we pass in the hallways," she says, "you won't keep ducking your head or looking away?"

"I haven't been—" I start to say, but she puts a finger to her lips and goes, "Shhh." Next, she leans forward, kisses me on the forehead like I'm her brother, and goes back to sit with Colin.

x x x

Hey you—

I didn't think this day would ever come, but it's finally here. Tryouts start tomorrow—or today, since it's two twenty in the morning. I NEED to sleep, but I've spent the last hour staring at the ceiling. I know I've told you that

I'm playing for both of us, that I'm bringing your spirit with me, and I will, but the flesh-and-blood, living and breathing you should be there. We should walk into that gym together.

Nate

24

DAY ONE ISN'T MUCH OF anything. Thirty-five guys turn out, but a dozen will end up on JV. The Champions guys all wear their Champions T-shirts and hang together. They might as well have a sign over their heads saying We're on the Team.

Coach Smiley sticks numbers on our backs and gets us into groups of five. Then he tells us to breathe slowly, clear our minds. The returning varsity players laugh because Smiley is *always* telling people to breathe slowly and clear their minds. After that, it's chest passes and bounce passes, right hand lay-ins and left hand lay-ins, midrange jumpers and three-pointers, dribbling through cones with the left hand, dribbling through cones with the right. At the tail end, there's a short scrimmage. I do okay, but so does everybody else.

On day two, Varner tells us to form groups of three, and I know I'm in trouble. I haven't hung out with anybody since Nooksack, so while other guys team up, I stand around looking at my shoes.

I end up stuck with Wally Harter and Greg Domingo. They're both okay players—but just barely okay. I panic—how can I show what I've got with these two as partners.

I know what I should do—respect the game no matter who my teammates are. If they can't handle my pass, if they don't use my screen—it doesn't matter. Play the right way.

I know it, but I don't do it. Instead, I take too many shots, make too few passes, and let my bad offense turn into bad defense. With Varner and Smiley watching, we don't just lose, we get trounced.

At the end of our fourth rotation, Domingo gets in my face. "Dravus," he says, "how about passing the ball once in a while?"

"I will. I will," I say, but in the next game I play the same stupid way. The way water circles around after you flush the toilet? That's me. I'm spinning downward, and I can't stop. We play two more games and get our heads handed to us two more times. When Varner blows the whistle, Harter and Domingo knuckle bump one another but turn their backs on me.

Late that night, with sleep impossible, I go to my window and look across the street toward Lucas's house. No sound of a basketball being dribbled, no shadow players—just the streetlight, the swaying branches, the crooked hoop hammered into the tree, and silence.

At Crown Hill, I dived for loose balls, fought through screens, blocked out on rebounds, looked for open teammates. I never thought about points. That player could make the team. The ME-ME-ME guy who was out there today has no chance. One more day to make good on my promise to Lucas. I take a breath, go back to bed, and sleep.

25

FIRST THING ON DAY THREE, Varner calls out twenty names—sophomores and juniors—and they go off with Coach Rodriguez to compete for spots on the JV team. That was me last year, but seniors can't play JV.

Sixteen of us are left. Varner hands red jerseys to Colin, Charles, Manny, Arthur Jacobson, Flynn Westwood, and three other guys from Champions. The rest of us get green jerseys.

"Five on five, today," Varner says. "Full-court scrimmage. If you're wearing a green jersey, show me you can play against varsity athletes. If you've got a red jersey, prove I didn't make a mistake."

During warm-ups, I stretch, shoot a few midrange jumpers, a couple of bank shots from inside the paint, and some free throws. I don't put up a single three-pointer or try any flashy reverse lay-ins.

Smiley coaches my team. He must remember me from

last year's JV–varsity game because he makes me his starting point guard, matching me up against Colin. It's as if he's saying *Okay, kid, here's your chance to show that game wasn't a fluke.*

Before the scrimmage begins, all the crazy impulses from yesterday rush back. I picture myself making steals, driving the lane for flashy lay-ins, swishing ridiculous three-pointers.

Nate Dravus—STAR!

That's when Lucas starts talking to me. *NO! NO! NO!* I hear him say, and I listen. On our first possession, I pass up a chance for a steal, get in solid defensive position, guarding Colin tight but not so tight he can blow by me. He gives me a stutter step; I cut him off. He passes.

I did nothing, I think. But then it hits me—he did nothing. I don't have to outplay him; I need to hold him in check while getting a couple of hoops, assists, and rebounds of my own. That's enough to prove that I belong.

The game flows. Colin gets a hoop on a fifteen-footer, but my hand was in his face. I make a sweet backdoor pass to Wally Harter. Harter blows the lay-in, but I made the right play.

Smiley helps me. When Colin comes out, he takes me out. When Colin goes back in, I'm back in. Colin fakes me out and drives to the hoop for a bucket. Lucas wouldn't panic, so I don't. I deflect a couple of Colin's passes and get a hand in his face on two other shots—both misses. I clank a fifteen-foot jumper of my own from the wing but hit my next shot from the same spot. Solid, steady basketball.

The session is just about over when I think, *Okay, look for a chance to do something great.* Even as I'm thinking it, I know it's a mistake, but the thought sticks.

I bring the ball into forecourt. Patrick Colligan posts up, and I feed him a bounce pass. Colin collapses on Colligan, double-teaming him, so I spot up for a corner three. Patrick sees me, makes the pass, but it's high and wide, nearly taking me out-of-bounds. No chance to get up a shot.

Colin is on me, his hands slapping at the ball. Manny joins him, double-teaming me. I should get the ball back to Colligan, who is unguarded, but I see space between Colin and Manny. I spin toward the opening, thinking to split the double-team, drive to the hoop, and score a bucket that will secure my spot on the varsity.

My shoulders slip through, but as I try to dribble, my feet get tangled and I lose my balance. I get my hands down so I don't do a face-plant, but the ball bounces away, and Charles snatches it up. Colin has taken off, and Charles hits him in stride. From the gym floor I watch Colin take two dribbles, then soar into the air for a thunderous slam dunk. The guys on the Red team roar and punch each other in awe. The whistle blows. Game over. Tryouts over.

x x x

Hey Lucas—

I MADE THE TEAM! It was by the skin of my teeth, but I made it, and that's what matters. Varner posted the roster today. I read down the list of ten typed names—Colin, Charles, Manny—all the guys you'd expect, but not me. Below the typed list, in shaky, old-man's handwriting, were two more names, mine and Patrick Colligan's. Varner spelled my name Dravis, so I got out my pencil and changed the i to u, making it official.

After school I stopped by Varner's office to pick up my uniform and the schedule, and I got more great news. Varner has the team entered in a Christmas tournament in Victoria, British Columbia. That means I'll be gone for three days of my Grandfather Frick's visit. He was a judge in Montana, and I feel for anybody who was in his court. Grandmother Frick might be just as mean, but she doesn't say much. Missing out on three days of Grandfather Frick is the best Christmas gift I'll get. It didn't seem like you had grandparents, or if you did, they never visited. FYI: That isn't all bad.

After I told my parents I'd made varsity, they took me to Red Mill for dinner, and then they said they wanted to buy me new basketball shoes, which made me think of you and your duct-taped shoes.

They would have taken me to Fleet Feet, but I told them Big 5 was fine. I found a Steph Curry model—not the crazy expensive ones with the wild colors—just regular black-and-white basketball shoes. And get this—they were two for one, so I'll have one pair for practice, and I can keep another pair strictly for games.

Back home, I brought the shoes upstairs to my room, got out a red Sharpie, took out the insoles, wrote **Lucas** on the flip side of one insole and **Cawley** on the flip side of the other, and then put them back in, right side up. When I'm running the court, you're running the court.

Nate

26

THERE IS A PEP RALLY today in the gym, pumping up the student body for the basketball season. Hanna introduces the girls' team first, and there is the normal cheering as Coach Reilley calls the names of each of her players.

When that's over, Colin introduces Coach Varner. As Varner walks up to the microphone, the cheer team unfurls two long banners, one at each end of the gym. The east banner has a picture of Varner in the center, with the words THANKS FOR 37 YEARS! written below. At the west end, the banner has the same picture of Varner, but reads THIS YEAR . . . HIS TIME!

Varner gets so choked up he can't talk, so Colin has everybody chant "METRO TITLE . . . METRO TITLE . . ." with clap clap clap-clap-clap in the middle. Teachers come out of the bleachers and hug Varner, a bunch of them crying. Varner never does speak.

x x x

Hey you—

Here's how things stand. I'm on the team, but I'm not really on the team. I warm up, do the drills and the walk-throughs of defensive and offensive plays, just like everybody else. Once we scrimmage, though, I'm stuck standing on the side of the court next to Patrick Colligan, watching.

Flynn Westwood's play is driving me crazy. You know him—he's the kid who wears a red headband to keep his shoulder-length black hair from flopping into his eyes. He was second string last year and he's second string this year, and it doesn't bother him at all.

The guy is decent on offense, but he sucks on defense. When he guards Colin in scrimmages, he plays soft, and Colin beats him like a drum. Smiley and Varner yell out instructions: "Take away his driving lane!" or "Make him dribble!" Flynn tightens up for a few plays, and then it's same-old, same-old.

A couple of times I've seen Varner and Smiley look over at me and talk. I think Smiley's telling Varner to give me a shot, but it hasn't happened yet. My parents and Amelia tell me to sit tight, be patient, wait my turn . . . all the stuff you hear all the time. I nod and say, "Yeah, yeah, yeah," but what I really want to do is scream. I'm glad the Thanksgiving break is coming up—it'll give me a break from standing along the sidelines doing nothing.

I can't see your mom or Bill cooking a turkey, and I can't picture Sara and Richard cooking one either. They'll probably get a couple of rotisserie chickens from Safeway. Whatever they do, they'll miss you.

Nate

27

AMELIA COMES HOME FOR THANKSGIVING. We don't talk much until Sunday, when we do miniature golf, again in the rain, but this time she beats me.

"How's your head?" she asks on the ride home.

"What do you mean?" I say.

"You know what I mean. You're on the team, and Lucas Cawley isn't. That's got to be hard."

"Yeah," I admit. "It is."

"How's Colin handling it? You talk to him about Lucas?"

I go light in the head. Talk to Colin about Lucas?

"Sometimes," I manage.

"That's good," she says, "because he's going through the same things you are, though I still think you should see a counselor."

For a millisecond I consider telling her that I don't need a counselor, because I tell Lucas what's going on, but if I admitted that, she'd *really* want me to go see a shrink, so I keep my mouth shut.

Hey you—

I know, it's been weeks. I kept putting off writing because I keep waiting for something to break for me, but nothing has.

The team has played six games and has won them all. I've been on the court for a grand total of eight minutes, all in garbage time. The games have been against mediocre teams, but they've been close, which has Varner steamed. "You're sleepwalking," he keeps saying. "You're going to get slapped in the face when you play a top team."

I wouldn't admit this to anyone but you, but I'm hoping for a slap-in-the-face big-time loss, because as long as we keep winning, I keep sitting.

One good thing has happened. You know how when you're shooting around to loosen up and you half guard a guy? Colin used to do that with Flynn Westwood, but he gave me a nod a week ago that said, "You ready?" It surprised me, and it ticked off Flynn, but I was ready.

Since then, we find a side hoop and for the ten minutes before practice starts, it's game on. That day you and me took on Colin and Bo in front of my house? It's like that, back and forth, back and forth, with one change—Colin doesn't call any ticky-tack fouls. It's straight-up hoops.

Last thing—that trip to Victoria? The athletic department pays the expenses for only eight players. Coach Varner said he wished it was different, but the only way I could go would be to pay my own way.

The ferry, hotels, food, and everything—the total comes to way over a thousand bucks. I don't have the money, not after paying my parents back for Champions, and I can't ask them to pay for me to sit on the bench. So I'll be listening to Grandfather Frick make his snide comments after all.

Nate

28

CHRISTMAS EVE STARTS OUT OKAY. Amelia is home, and my parents use Chromecast to put her Cal–Stanford soccer match on the TV, my dad replaying Amelia's winning goal about ten times. Amelia's embarrassed, but it takes the pressure off me.

Then it all goes bad.

Once the TV gets turned off, Grandfather Frick asks me if I'm playing any sport. My mom jumps in to tell him how proud she is that I'd made the varsity basketball team.

Grandfather Frick starts in with the questions, asking what position I play, how many points I score. To get it over with, I tell him I'm a benchwarmer. He gives his little chuckle and tells me that maybe I should have taken up bowling.

I'm thinking that's the worst of it, but while everybody else is discussing an ice storm in Portland, he's checking his phone.

"It says here," he blurts out, "that yesterday Shilshole High lost 66–47 in the championship game in a tournament in British Columbia. Isn't that your school?"

My dad explains that only eight players go to tournaments.

Grandfather Frick chuckles again. "So, you're a benchwarmer who doesn't even have a seat on the bench. That's a new one."

"Enough," my dad says, angry.

"It's okay," I say.

"It's not okay," my mom says. Then she turns to Grandfather Frick. "You're going to apologize to Nate," she says.

Grandfather gives his chuckle again. "What? The boy can't take a little joke?"

"Jokes are only funny if they're funny for everyone," my mom says.

Grandmother Frick, who has been silent as usual, speaks up. "Dear, you were a little out of line."

He shrugs and says he's sorry, that he meant no harm, but people were tougher in his time. When he finishes, Amelia leaves the room, so I do the same.

x x x

Hey you—

I got an email from Coach Varner saying that Coach Smiley tested positive for Covid when he got back from Victoria. Varner says Smiley feels fine and will be back soon, but practices have been canceled for this week and we should all take Covid tests.

Our next game is away against Garfield. They've dozens of Metro titles, including last year. Playing them in their gym without practicing for a week—it could be ugly.

Nate

29

GARFIELD CRUSHES US 82-56, AND the game isn't that close. My parents are in the stands to watch me play my paltry two minutes, miss the one shot I take, and snag a single rebound. The ride home is quiet.

Before practice today, Varner has us sit on the floor while he paces back and forth, chewing us out. "Not enough toughness. Not enough heart."

Guys hang their heads, and I hang mine, but I'm thinking, *Don't blame me, I hardly played.*

He stops. "Any ideas," he says, "on how we can get some grit?"

A long wait, and then I hear Colin. "When we're warming up, Dravus guards me so tight I can smell the salami sub he had for lunch."

Guys snicker, but Varner flashes a look that stops all laughter. "Meaning?" he says.

Colin shrugs. "If I hate going up against him, then guys on the other team would hate it, too."

I can't believe what I'm hearing. Colin speaking up for me?

Flynn Westwood turns on him. "You saying I don't play tough defense?"

"No—" Colin begins, but Varner cuts him off.

"Zip it," he says, "both of you."

Heads go down.

"Anybody else got anything?" Varner asks.

Heads stay down, but every nerve in my body is on alert.

During our drills, the gym crackles with the tension between Colin and Westwood. When Varner goes over defensive tweaks, he calls me out to demonstrate how to go over screens and how to switch. He's sizing me up, and Westwood's eyes are boring a hole in me, but I focus on basketball.

Finally it's time to scrimmage. I'm hoping I'll be out there in place of Westwood, but as usual, I start on the sideline, watching.

Westwood has something to prove. First possession, he gets right up on Colin—too tight. Colin feeds Charles on the post and then cuts backdoor to the hoop for a lay-in, making Westwood look foolish.

That bucket is gas on the fire. As Westwood brings the ball into forecourt, Colin establishes a solid defensive position. There's no place for Westwood to go, but he drives to the hoop anyway, throwing up a wild shot that barely grazes iron.

That's how it goes for the first half of the scrimmage, Westwood trying so hard to be great that he's awful. Finally, Varner stops the scrimmage and looks at me. "Take Flynn's spot," he says.

I play the rest of the scrimmage, and I play tough. I shoulder

Colin as he dribbles, get a hand in his face when he shoots, keep my elbows out to screen him off the boards. Nothing dirty, nothing crazy. Okay, maybe one crazy thing. I feel Lucas with me, helping me. When Varner blows the whistle ending practice, I'm on the court, drenched in sweat.

As I head to the locker room, Westwood bumps me. I pretend I don't notice. Colin is off to my right. I consider thanking him for what he said, but then I'm back at Nooksack, seeing his grinning face as he pushes the canoe out into the river, and that thought is gone.

Nathan Hale tomorrow in their gym. The way horses snort and stomp the ground before the start of the Kentucky Derby—that's me. I'm ready.

x x x

Hey you—

YES! YES! YES! YES!

It happened! All those people telling me to be patient—they were right. First quarter the starters play tough defense and push the ball on offense. Colin hits a pull-up jumper, a driving lay-in; Manny drops in a three-pointer from the corner. With two minutes left in the quarter, Varner pulls Colin for a rest. He looks right past Westwood and points at me—my first non-garbage minutes all year.

I'm amped, my heart pounding, my hands sweaty. I remember Smiley's advice and take deep breaths.

Nothing special happens when I'm on the court. I feed

Charles the ball on the post, get Manny an open shot in the corner. On defense, I keep my guy in check and slap a lazy pass out-of-bounds. When I took the court, we were up by five points. When Varner puts Colin back in, we're up by seven.

I stay in the rotation, getting minutes in every quarter. I harass whichever Hale guy I'm guarding, trying to get into his head the way I got into biker-guy Craig's. I make a steal, score on a driving lay-in, and a minute later knock down an open shot from the free throw line.

Charles and Arthur Jacobson go off in the third quarter, scoring fourteen points between them. We're crushing Hale by twenty points with four minutes left, when Varner empties his bench, giving Westwood the garbage time I used to get.

Westwood is scowling when he checks in. The first time he touches the ball, he lets fly a twenty-five-footer. Airball. Varner and Smiley holler at him, but he doesn't even look over. Next time down, he heaves up another long-distance three. This one hits the back iron. Hale grabs the long rebound and turns it into an easy fast break bucket. Varner jumps up, pointing at me. "Take Westwood's place!"

I hustle to the scorer's table and check in on the next dead ball. We're up by eighteen points, but I play those last minutes as if I'm in game seven of the NBA finals. I score four points, get an assist, deflect two passes, and block a shot.

Relentless, like you.

After we shake hands with the Hale guys, Flynn elbows past me on our way into the locker room. "Move it, Dravus," he says. He's still looking for a fight, but I just move out of his way. He's in my rearview mirror; I've got my eyes focused on Colin up ahead.

If I told that to anybody but you, they'd say I was in la-la land, and I get that. Colin was second team all-league last year. He worked all spring and summer with Champions. He's the captain of the team. Varner trusts him.

All that's on his side. On my side are the workouts at home, the hours at Crown Hill, the coaching I got from Trey, and my Steph Curry shoes with your name in them. So, yeah, it's a long shot, but it's a shot.

x x x

Nate

Hey you—

We've won four more games. Okay, the teams we played have all been bottom dwellers, but a win is a win. Right now, we're in a first-place tie with Lakeshore and North Central in the North Division. I'm playing so much I've had to rewrite your name in my shoes because the letters got smudged out by the sweat from my feet.

That link with Charles that I had at Champions? I've still got it. I just know when he's looking for a lob over the top or when he wants to post his guy up or when he wants me to set a screen. My feel for Manny isn't as good, but it's getting better.

Our next game—Rainier Beach—will be a big test. Right now, they're tied with Garfield for first place in the South. Someone said that Coach Varner has never beaten Rainier Beach in all his years of coaching, which is hard to believe. After thirty-seven years, you'd think he'd have at least one victory.

The game is Friday night, and our gym will be packed. My parents are going to be there, and Amelia called to say that she wished she could see the game, too. I heard my mom talking to my dad about telling Grandfather Frick how much I'm playing, but my dad told her to let it go.

Nate

30

THE RAINIER BEACH PLAYERS KNOW that Garfield stomped us, so they figure they'll do the same. They play loose and wild in the first half, racing up and down the court, jacking up shots from long distance, not bothering to block out on the boards. Their coach is going crazy on the sideline, yelling "Focus! Focus! Focus!" over and over. Here's the thing, though. They're so good that even though they're playing badly, they're still beating us.

"Stay close," Varner says during time-outs and the breaks between quarters. "Make it to the fourth quarter, and anything can happen."

I get my normal minutes, subbing for Colin when he needs a rest. I'm hyper-focused, channeling Lucas when I'm on defense. The whole team is in beast mode, fighting for every loose ball and getting most of them. At the start of the fourth quarter, we're within three.

Beach's best player is a tall kid with huge hands, DeSean Royce, who is headed to Gonzaga. He's got it all—a soft shooting touch and a lightning-fast crossover, and he can jump out of the gym.

With three minutes left in the game, DeSean anticipates a pass, makes a clean steal, and breaks for the hoop. Manny, a step behind, goes up with him, swipes at the ball, misses, but his open hand rakes DeSean across the eyes, sending him to the ground.

The ref blows his whistle, calls the foul on Manny, and then steps to the side and confers with the other ref. I can't figure what they're talking about, but Smiley knows. "He was going for the ball!" he shouts.

The refs walk to the scorer's table. "Flagrant foul," one of them says. "Number seventeen is ejected."

Manny's mouth drops open, but before he can argue, Smiley leads him off the court.

Varner calls my name. "Don't worry about scoring," he says as I step onto the court. "That'll be on Colin and Charles. Just don't give Royce anything easy."

Being Colin's teammate throws me off. At Salmon Bay K–8, I *always* played against him. Last year, when Lucas and I were on JV, he was on varsity. At Champions and on this year's varsity, whenever I was on the court, he was resting on the bench. I know being teammates throws him off, too, because he gives me a look that says, *How do we even do this?*

The whistle blows, and I stop worrying about Colin and

lock in on DeSean Royce, but after Royce makes one of his free throws, pushing their lead to four, the Beach coach pulls him so their trainer can check him over.

With Royce on the bench, Charles takes over. I get him the ball on a lob over the top. He catches it and—in one motion— dunks it, and our fans are screaming. Next possession, after a Rainier Beach miss, I feed Charles the ball again. This time he backs his guy down, spins, hits a turnaround jumper, and is fouled. When he sinks the free throw, we're up one, and the roof is about to come off the gym.

The Beach coach calls time to set up a play. When they break the huddle, DeSean is back in. They isolate him against me; I get right up in his face, ready—I think. And then he's by me and the backboard is rattling from his dunk.

Rainier Beach by one with twelve seconds left.

Now Varner calls time, and we huddle as he draws up a play on his whiteboard, screaming to be heard above the roar of the crowd. I'm to feed the ball to Charles, who will suck in the defense and then kick the ball back to me. Colin will fake a backdoor cut, then pop into the corner. "If Colin is open," Varner says to me, "get him the ball. If not, you take the final shot. Bryce, Arthur—you two hit the boards. Everybody got it?"

We nod. The horn sounds.

Colin inbounds to me. Charles posts, and I feed him the ball. Colin's man drops down to double-team, and Charles passes the ball back out to me. Colin breaks hard toward the hoop, then stops on a dime and spots up in the corner. He's wide-open, clapping his hands, calling for the ball. The crowd has been counting down the seconds . . . "Six . . . Five . . . Four . . ." He's a good shooter, he's got a clean look, and I've got time.

I know the right play, but I don't make it.

Instead, I take a hard dribble toward the hoop and pull up for a fifteen-footer. A defender is on me, his hand in my face. Somehow I get the shot off, but the ball barely draws iron; Rainier Beach snags the rebound; the horn sounds.

Game over.

As the Beach guys high-five one another, Colin and Bryce and Arthur head to the bench. Charles, though, stands perfectly still, hands on his hips, staring me down.

I take my time walking home, hoping my parents will be in bed, but they're up. They say that taking the final shot took courage and that they're proud of me, but they saw Colin wide-open in the corner.

Everybody saw him.

x x x

Hey you—

What can I say? I blew it. I went rogue in the last seconds against Rainier Beach, throwing away a game we should have won. That rumor about Varner having never beaten Rainier Beach? It's true, and it's still true—all because of me.

The team has played twice since then, both victories, but I haven't played at all, not even in garbage time. Colin has been on the court for almost the entire game. When he does come out, it's Patrick Colligan who goes in. I'm down at the end of the bench next to Flynn Westwood. Varner never looks at either of us, and neither does Smiley.

We play Lakeshore next, that rich kid school up by Shoreline. They've got two guards in the top five in the league in scoring, Miller Doakes and R.J. Greene. Right now, Lakeshore is tied with us and North Central for first place in the North Division. If we win one of our next two games, we make the playoff for the North Division crown. We lose them both, and our season is over.

Everybody else is amped, and I'm trying to keep positive, but it's hard. We were there—you and me—a major part of the team. All I had to do was make the right play, and we'd still be there. It's on me, and I'm sorry.

After I put this notebook away, I'll try to watch one of our shadow games, but lately I can't pick out you or me or anybody. The shadows are just shadows.

Nate

31

HOW'S THIS FOR A START in a crucial game? On our first possession against Lakeshore, Manny goes up for a rebound and comes down on Arthur Jacobson's foot, rolling his ankle.

Our trainer, Mr. Kelly, runs out and hovers over him. Manny's got his hands covering his face and is rocking his head back and forth. After a couple of minutes, Kelly helps him up, and with Charles supporting one shoulder and Colin the other, Manny hobbles off the court.

I'm on the bench thinking, *Put me in!* but Varner calls out Patrick Colligan's name.

I don't mean to diss Colligan. He's a good guy, and he gives it his all, but he's slow. He's done okay subbing for Colin a minute here and there. But a full game against a top opponent?

Colligan is supposed to guard Doakes, but Doakes scores on three straight possessions, two blow-bys and one long bomb. Varner calls time. I'm thinking/hoping he'll put me in, but he doesn't. "Deep breaths," Smiley says to Colligan as he goes back out.

Colligan must not breathe deep enough, because on the next possession, Doakes picks his pocket, and Lakeshore scores on a fast break. After that, Colligan plays better, and Charles gets hot, but at the half Lakeshore's lead is fourteen.

I'm thinking Varner has *got* to put me in, but Colligan starts the third quarter. When Doakes cools off, R.J. Greene catches fire, knocking down two triples.

One minute into the fourth quarter, when Lakeshore's lead reaches twenty-two, their coach pulls his starters. They grin and high-five one another before taking a seat on the bench to watch the subs finish us off.

That's when Varner finally calls my name. I think he's going to pull all the starters and have me out there with Westwood and Colligan and those guys, but he doesn't. Colin stays in, along with Charles, Bryce Chambers, and Arthur Jacobson.

We start clicking—sharp passes, quick cuts, solid defense. It's against their second team, but so what? With four minutes left, the lead is down to twelve.

Lakeshore's coach reinserts his starters, but their heads aren't in the game, and we have all the momentum. I play Lucas Cawley defense, completely shutting down Doakes.

With two minutes left, Lakeshore's lead is six. They isolate Doakes on me. The shot clock is ticking down. Four . . . three . . . two. I'm all over him, right in his jersey, as he lets loose a desperation heave from the top of the key. The ball hits the front rim, climbs three feet, and somehow drops down and through. Pure luck—but Lakeshore's lead is back to nine, and there just isn't enough time.

We lose 79–73, but I've got to believe I'm out of Varner's dog-house. The North Central game is win or go home. Varner's last year; Varner's last chance.

My last chance, too.

32

TODAY AT LUNCH, CHARLES COMES over and sits with me. "You're going to start against North Central," he says.

"How do you know?" I say, fighting to hide my excitement.

"Because Manny won't be ready," he says. "The swelling is so bad you can't even see his ankle."

He motions with his head to his table. "Come eat with the guys. Don't sit over here alone."

I scrunch up my face and shake my head. "I'm almost done," I say.

As he stands, he grabs the top of my shirt and gives it a tug. "Come on," he says, so I go.

Colin is talking with Hanna at the opposite end of the table. She smiles at me; Colin's face stays blank. Manny is right across from me. I give him a fist bump. Somebody asks about his ankle. "Getting better," he says. "I think I'll be ready for North Central."

I listen as the guys talk about who should make the NBA

All-Star team. I want to join in, but I can't find the moment, and I'm out of practice. I put my head down and eat.

x x x

Hey you—

I don't know why, but tonight I keep thinking about you being Creepy Crawley for all those years. I know—random—but you can't control the stuff that comes into your head.

You must have thought about ditching Megan and hanging out with the rest of us. The brothers and sisters of other kids in her class did that, but you stuck with her. I don't know if I would have done that if she were my sister. In fact, I'm pretty sure I wouldn't have.

North Central tomorrow. Win or go home.

Nate

Hey you—

When I got to the gym and Coach Smiley came over, I was preparing myself to hear that Manny was ready to go, but it was the opposite. "You're starting," he said. "Just breathe and clear your mind, and you'll be fine."

I was psyched to take the court, but this was Coach Varner's last home game, so there was a goodbye ceremony. The principal, the athletic director, and most of the Shilshole teachers were there, and so was the mayor of Seattle. They made short speeches praising Varner, and then about fifty former players came to center court to present him with a plaque that'll go up outside the gym. It reads Henry Varner Gymnasium.

I thought the hoopla was over, but Varner's family came out next. Varner hugged his wife and kids and grandkids before taking the microphone. You could see he was emotional, but he managed to thank everybody. At the end he looked over at the refs and said, "That includes you." The whole gym erupted into laughter as if it was the funniest thing they'd ever heard.

It would suck to lose with all those people there, but when the game started, I was tight as a drum and so was the rest of the team. North Central took advantage and jumped out to a six-point lead. Varner called time, but he was still teary-eyed, so it was Smiley who talked to us. "Close your eyes," he says, "and go to your place of peace. When you open your eyes, play the way you know how."

We smiled at one another, and maybe that is what broke the tension. When I stepped back onto the court, I FELT AMAZING. It was as if I was in one of our shadow games where everything goes right. The basket was the size of a Hula-Hoop; North Central's players were moving in slow motion. My shots dropped; my passes were pinpoint, especially to Charles. I just *knew* what move he was going to make, and I got him the ball on time in rhythm. I was okay with Colin, getting him the ball when he was open, keeping him involved.

I was so deep in the zone that time didn't exist. It

wasn't until the horn sounded and Colligan gave me a breather that I looked at the scoreboard. The first quarter was almost over. We weren't down six anymore—we were up seven.

Colligan stayed on the court for the first minute of the second quarter. When I returned, I was thinking, I won't be in the same zone—BUT I WAS!

For the entire game I was shooting lights out, making great passes. On defense, I got a couple of steals and pulled down more than my share of rebounds. The crowd was roaring as our lead grew and grew.

Three minutes into the fourth quarter, we were up nineteen. I snatched a rebound, pushed the ball up court, and fed Charles for a slam dunk. He was fouled, and as he stepped to the free throw line, the horn sounded. Colligan came back in to take my spot. As I walked off the court, the entire side of our gym was standing and chanting: "NATE! NATE! NATE!" but in my head I was shouting LUCAS! LUCAS! LUCAS! because you were with me.

Nate

33

IT'S BEEN CRAZY AROUND MY house since the North Central game. My mom filmed it, and then my dad edited it down to the highlights, which he sent to Amelia. She called, and when I answered, she chanted, "NATE! NATE! NATE!" After dinner, I heard my mom talking to Grandfather Frick, and I knew what she was talking about.

I can't keep reliving that game. I've got to focus on the next one. The Metro League cut back on playoff games during Covid, and they've kept it that way. Now it's the top four teams, single elimination. Friday—two days from now—while we're playing Lakeshore for the North Division title, Rainier Beach will take on Garfield in the South. Sunday, it's North versus South for the Metro title. What used to take two weeks wraps up in one weekend.

I get little-kid-at-Disneyland goose bumps thinking about knocking off Lakeshore and then playing for the Metro title. I know you're never supposed to think past the next game, but maybe coaches say that because everybody does it.

× × ×

Hey Lucas—

Hold on tight because you're going on a wild ride.

A storm blew down from Canada, and it was going strong when we took the court against Lakeshore. During warm-ups, the lights flickered a couple of times.

My parents arrived an hour early, so even though the gym was packed, they were sitting right behind our bench. As I was shooting layups, my dad gave me a thumbs-up that I pretended not to see.

Before the game, Varner pulled me aside. "Manny's starting," he told me. "A player doesn't lose his position by injury, not on my teams, but he's on limited minutes. Be ready."

My heart sank a little. I wanted my mom and dad to hear my name over the PA system. Starting for Shilshole High—Nate Dravus. I wanted it for you, too. That would have been awesome.

Then I thought—Stealth Bomber—and I was okay.

From the opening tip, the Lakeshore defense double-teamed Charles and Colin, forcing other guys to shoot.

Manny saw what was happening and looked to score. He's not a great shooter, but you leave him open and he'll knock down his share. Jacobson and Chambers were tentative, but they made a bucket here and there. For Lakeshore, it was the Miller Doakes and R.J. Greene show. I subbed for Colin at the end of the first quarter but was back on the bench as Lakeshore built a six-point lead.

Halfway through the second quarter, Manny was winded, sucking air every chance he got. Next trip down, he telegraphed a pass to Colin that Doakes deflected toward center court. R.J. Greene scooped up the ball, drove to the hoop, and rose for a dunk that would have brought the Lakeshore crowd into a frenzy.

Only it all went wrong.

Greene misjudged his jump, jamming the ball against the front of the rim. When he came down, his legs flew out from under him, and he fell hard, smacking first his back and then his head against the gym floor with a sickening thud. Everybody gasped, and then the gym went silent as the Lakeshore trainer and coach raced out to check on him. A moment later they were joined by a woman, saying, "I'm a doctor. I'm a doctor," over and over. Players on both teams took a knee.

Finally, Greene struggled to his feet. The crowd started clapping, quietly at first, and then louder and louder as he made his way into the locker room.

We huddled around Varner. "All right," he said. "A doctor is with their guy. You saw him walk off. He's going to be okay. So focus on the game. You hear me? Focus."

Everybody nodded, but for the rest of the half, both teams went through the motions, doing nothing. The crowd stayed hushed, too. It felt more like a PE scrimmage than a playoff game. At halftime, Lakeshore was up seven.

In the locker room, Varner and Smiley talked before Varner went to the chalkboard. The plan was simple. With Greene out, Doakes was their main threat, so we switched to a box-and-one defense. Four guys in a zone, with one guy man-to-man on Doakes, hounding him. That one guy was me. The whole Stealth Bomber plan was coming true.

"Don't worry about fouling out," Varner told me, "because you've got Manny backing you up. Make Doakes miserable."

Once I was on the court, I jumped up and down a few times, feeling both those Steph Curry game shoes and your name, and I was ready.

I hounded Doakes everywhere he went, just like you would have. Even during dead balls I stayed next to him, getting in his head. If he moved away, I moved with him. You couldn't tell my sweat from his.

My focus was on defense, but I did okay on offense. I missed Colin a couple of times when he was open, but I made two good passes to Charles, and he converted both.

We erased their lead halfway into the third quarter. Their coach called time-out, but when their huddle broke, I was right there, inches from Doakes as he walked toward center court.

"Back off," he snarled, sounding just like biker-guy Craig.

When I didn't, he gave me a shove. The ref saw it and T'ed him up. I sank the free throw, and their coach sat Doakes down to cool him off. When he returned to the game, I was back in his jersey. I got three fouls called on me, but he was so mad at me that his game was way off.

R.J. Greene returned to the Lakeshore bench in street clothes at the start of the fourth quarter. The crowd cheered like crazy, and Lakeshore went on a little run, but Colin hit a three-pointer to push our lead to twelve. Manny took my place halfway through the fourth quarter and finished the game, which was okay by me because I was exhausted. We won by fifteen.

On the ride home, my parents were bubbling with excitement the way they did when Amelia had had a big game. That went on for about ten minutes, and then it was as if everyone hit a wall, and silence took over.

Winning was great—I'm not going to pretend it wasn't. But in that silence, one thought kept circling in my head, and it's still circling.

You should have been on the court, and Bill and Megan and Richard and Sara and even your mom should have been in the stands cheering for you. On the ride back to your home, they should have told you how great you played and how happy you made them feel. All the good stuff that's come my way? You should have had it, too.

Day off tomorrow—no practice or anything. Varner says we should stay away from basketball, which I won't be able to do. The Metro title game is Sunday night in the Rainier Beach gym. When I put this notebook away, I'll get my red Sharpie out and rewrite your name, big and bold, inside my shoes. I'm going to need you.

Nate

34

THIS MORNING I GET A text from Charles, which surprises me because I didn't know he had my number.

"Hoops at GG at noon?" it reads.

I text back: "Y."

When I get to Golden Gardens, he's already there. As we're shooting around, he tells me that Manny's ankle ballooned after the game. "He's going to ice it," Charles says, "but who knows how long he'll be able to go."

I'm letting that sink in when I hear another ball being dribbled, look over, and see Colin heading our way. When he sees me, he stops for a second, surprised, but he keeps coming.

We do the knuckle bumps, and then Charles tells Colin the news about Manny. "So," Charles says when he finishes, "you two got something to say to each other?"

We both give him blank looks.

"Don't act dumb," he says. "I'm on the court." He points at

Colin. "You and me—we're in rhythm." He turns and points at me. "And so are we," he says. "With the two of you, everything is off. Something is there, between you, holding you back, and it's holding the team back."

No one speaks. The only sounds are the waves lapping up on the beach and dogs barking in the distance.

"I'm going over to Little Coney to get myself a burger, milkshake, and fries," Charles says, an edge in his voice. "You two work it out, whatever it is, because we have no chance—and I mean *no chance*—to beat Rainier Beach unless you do."

Once he's gone, Colin and I are left looking at one another.

"You got anything you want to say to me?" he asks.

"Not really," I say. "How about you?"

"Same," he answers.

We both look toward Little Coney, which Charles hasn't even reached. "He's going be a while," Colin says. "How about a game? HORSE? Twenty-one?"

"One-on-one," I say, because that's what we both want. "To eleven. Win by one."

"You got it," he says.

There is no pretending that it's a friendly game. He gives me the ball, and I go right at him, driving hard to the hoop and then hitting a step-back jumper. On his first possession he does the same thing to me, banking home a ten-footer.

That's how it goes, back and forth, nobody getting more than two ahead, until it's 10–10, and I've got the ball in my hands. I take a jab step to set up a fadeaway jump shot. I'm certain it's cash money, nothing but net, but Colin gets a fingertip on the ball. It hits short off the front rim; he clears the rebound and takes the ball to the far corner. I'm immediately on him—not a chance I'm going to give him an uncontested shot for the win. My hand is in his face as he goes up and releases. I turn, ready to rebound.

Swish.

"Again?" he asks.

"Again," I say.

We play two more games, and they're both tight, no give in either of us. He wins 11–7 and 11–9, but I'm not going to kid myself. He beat me fair and square, three times. No fluke shots, no luck involved. If we play ten times, I win two—max.

He's better.

We take a break, sit down. The wind is blowing through the trees; the sailboats are skimming on Puget Sound; the Olympic Mountains are peeking through the clouds.

"You ever think about him?" I say as a couple of kayakers come into view.

"Cawley?" he says. "Sure, I do. Not all the time like you do, but I think about him." He looks over at me. "I didn't kill him. I know you think I did, but I didn't."

"I don't think you killed him," I say.

"Yeah, you do," he says. "I see it in your eyes every time you look at me. The whole thing was Bo's idea, though once he told me, I was all in. Get you two in the canoe, give you a hard push toward the fast water, and then watch you get bounced around. A prank. That's all it was. Okay, maybe we were ticked that we were on the bench while you two finished the game, but we weren't trying to hurt anybody."

We both stare out at Puget Sound for a while, watching the waves, watching the kayakers, watching the sailboats.

"Explain something," he says at last. "I saw Cawley when they pulled him out of the river. He hadn't hit his head. He wasn't caught up in reeds or anything. He didn't have on heavy clothes or boots. All he had to do was swim ten yards, and he's on dry ground. I don't get how he drowned."

I'm at Golden Gardens, but in my head I'm back in front of my house. My mom has just asked Lucas if he wants to go to Pop Mounger Pool, and Lucas has said no and disappeared fast, and my mom is saying, "He might not know how to swim."

So that's what I tell Colin.

Colin's eyes go wide. "He didn't know how to swim?"

"You know what his parents were like," I say. "They wouldn't have signed up for classes."

"I don't know anything about his parents," he says. "You lived across the street from him, not me." Then he shakes his head. "He didn't know how to swim, but didn't say anything. He just got in a canoe and went out on a river? Why would he do that?"

"Come on, Colin," I say. "You think Creepy Crawley is going to turn to you and Bo and me and say, *I can't swim*? He's not going to do that."

Colin falls silent. He doesn't ask the next question; the question I've asked myself a thousand times.

Why didn't I say something?

Lucas was over there in his crappy house with Bill and Megan and his alcoholic mother until I got him into basketball. I didn't do it because I felt sorry for him or wanted to be a good neighbor. I did it for me. I needed a warm body to practice against, and he was the only warm body around. If I'd left him alone, he'd have never heard of Champions, never gone to Nooksack. Okay, sure—he could have stood up for himself. I know that. But when he didn't, it was on me to stand up for him.

I'm thinking that there's nothing more to say when Colin turns toward me. "Shouldn't we do something," he says, "to remember Cawley? Wear a black armband or something? I've wondered about it all season."

I tell him that I've got Lucas's name written inside my shoes.

"Okay with you if I do that, too?" he asks.

"Yeah," I say, "it's okay by me."

"Should we make it a team thing?" he asks. "Get everybody involved?"

"No," I say. "It was just us at Nooksack."

When Charles returns, he looks first at me, then at Colin. "You two good?" he says.

"I don't know about good," I say, "but we're better."

X X X

Hey Lucas—

I told Colin about writing your name on the insoles of my shoes. I know what you're thinking: Why would I tell him? All I can say is that it seemed like the right thing to do, so I did it, and I hope you can trust me on that. Shadows are going wild tonight, but I'm too pumped up to watch them. The season ends tomorrow.

Nate

35

WHEN I STEP INTO THE locker room before the title game, Colin motions me over to where he's sitting and shows me his shoes. He's got Lucas written on the insole of one of his shoes and Cawley on the insole of the other. "Like this?" he says, and I nod.

A couple of minutes later Manny comes in, not exactly limping, but not walking right either. I'm sorry he's hurt, but I'm pumped at the idea of getting some of his minutes.

We put on our uniforms; Varner gives his normal pep talk; Smiley tells us to breathe; we head out.

Until then, it's seemed like a regular game, but as soon as we step on the court, everything changes. Rainier Beach has won about fifty titles, both boys and girls, city and state, and all those banners are hanging from the rafters, crowding each other out. Their band is rocking the place with "Eye of the Tiger." Behind their bench is a large group of Black men—former Rainier Beach players who've come back for the game. I'm ninety percent sure one of them is Jamal Crawford, who played for something like twenty years in the NBA, and the others are college and NBA players, too. They're joking with one another, signing autographs, doing selfies with fans, being stars. I get goose bumps, and my spine is tingling.

I spot my parents in the stands, and I'm blown away to see Amelia sitting with them. She must have flown up from Berkeley just for this game. When our eyes catch, she stands and claps her hands above her head, and I can tell she's screaming "Nate! Nate! Nate!"

That quiet place Smiley talks about? GONE! A million sounds are roaring through my head and a gallon of adrenaline is racing through my bloodstream. We go through the layup line a few times, and then I hear, "Lucas! Over here."

Colin looks at me, confused. So does Charles. I give them my *I've got no clue* look until I see Trey, standing along the sidelines waving wildly to me.

When I go over, he holds up a piece of paper that has the rosters of both teams on it, points to the name across from my number, and asks who Nate Dravus is. I tell him it's complicated, and he shrugs and says, "Whatever, mate. Just be a Tasmanian devil."

I go back and finish the shoot around. The horn sounds, and the team huddles around Varner. He warns that Rainier Beach is going to come out on fire. "Hang in there," he says. "Weather the storm."

Manny starts, and I take the spot next to Smiley, one down from Varner. Varner's prediction is on the money. After Rainier Beach controls the tip, DeSean goes backdoor on Manny for a vicious dunk that shakes the backboard and brings the crowd to its feet.

It gets worse, fast. They trap Colin, make a steal, and score on a fast break. Then it's a miss by Charles followed by a corner three from one of their guards. After another miss, DeSean drives on Manny, gets fouled, but his shot finds the bottom of the net anyway. After he sinks the free throw, Beach is up 10–0, and the crowd smells blood.

Varner calls time to draw up a play. I'm hoping he's going to put me in, and I'm ready, but he sticks with Manny. I sit back on the bench, my knees bouncing up and down on their own.

Varner's play works perfectly. Charles pretends to pop out for a pass but instead cuts hard to the hoop. Colin hits him with a bounce pass, Charles rattles the backboard with a dunk, and it's our crowd—one-tenth the size of Beach's—that's up on their feet.

That basket settles us. We don't cut into Beach's lead, but it doesn't balloon. They're up by twelve, then eight, then ten, then seven, then nine. With two minutes left in the quarter, I sub in for Manny.

All season I've had a feel for Charles's game. The truth is I've always had a feel for Colin's game, too, but making the right play for him felt like a betrayal. Now we've both got the same thing written in our shoes. I know it's corny and hokey and all those things—but we're both playing for Lucas Cawley, so we've got to play together.

Rainier Beach tests me right away. First trip down, the guy I'm guarding puts his shoulder down and drives to the hoop. As he goes up, I swipe at the ball. I don't get it, but I foul him so hard across the arm that the shot has no chance. He misses the first foul shot short and the second one long, so it's a good foul.

Jacobson rebounds and passes the ball to me. In forecourt, we set up a triangle. I feed Charles, the ball comes back, Colin breaks for the basket and then pops into the corner. It's the play we ran in the final seconds of the first Rainier Beach game, but this time I make the pass and Colin drains the three-pointer. He points his finger at me, acknowledging the assist as we hustle back on defense.

I'm hoping Varner will leave me in, but when the second quarter starts, I'm back on the bench. Manny is playing through the pain, giving everything he's got, and the team hangs tough. Back out for the final minutes of the half, I go into my Tasmanian devil defense against DeSean.

With twenty seconds left, Beach isolates him against me. DeSean lets the clock run down before making his move. I slide over, blocking him, and there's a collision. I'm ninety percent certain my feet were set, but the ref calls the foul on me. DeSean hits both free throws; at half we're down eleven.

In the locker room, Varner makes some adjustments to our defense. I don't pay full attention because I'm watching our trainer, Mr. Kelly, retape Manny's ankle. Once Kelly finishes, Manny runs in place for a few seconds, wincing every time his left foot comes down.

I'm on the bench at the start of the third quarter. Halfway through the quarter, DeSean gives Manny a pump fake before driving hard to the hoop. Manny is right with him, and then he isn't. His ankle gives out as DeSean flushes the dunk. Varner is on his feet, calling time, Manny limps off, and I'm in the game for good.

I look at the scoreboard; we're halfway through the third quarter, with Beach leading by fourteen. I can see in their faces that they think they've got us. Their crowd feels the same way; they're cheering, but not as loudly. The man I think is Jamal Crawford has stayed, but most of the other NBA types have left.

A calm comes over me, maybe because for the first time all season I'm not fighting anybody on my team. Bryce Chambers is in, and he and Arthur Jacobson control the defensive boards and sneak in for an occasional offensive rebound. Charles, Colin, and I set up the triangle offense and work for a good shot.

I remember seeing a film of lava coming down the side of a mountain in Hawaii. That's how we are. We don't go on any crazy run and score ten straight. We're slow and steady, but relentless. We cut the fourteen-point lead to six, with six seconds left in the third quarter, only to see one of their guards sink a triple from the top of the key at the buzzer. But even that doesn't faze us.

In the fourth quarter, Beach slows the pace, hoping to thwart our comeback by milking the clock, but if you don't play at your regular pace, everything gets out of sync. We keep whittling away, eventually cutting the lead to four. The Rainier Beach crowd is back into the game, shaking the rafters with shouts of "DE-FENSE! DE-FENSE! DE-FENSE!"

The noise rattles me for a second, and in that second DeSean picks my pocket, races the length of the court, and soars for a slam dunk. I look at Colin, and he makes a fist signaling me to stay strong.

Next possession, Colin makes a spin move and I thread the needle with a bounce pass that he converts with a reverse lay-in, cutting the lead back to four with a little over a minute left.

Beach works for a good shot, but we play smothering defense—all of us Tasmanian devils. With the shot clock down to three, DeSean forces up a contested jump shot that misses badly. Jacobson clears the board and feeds me the outlet pass. I race the ball into the forecourt, drive toward the hoop, then kick a pass out to Charles, who's open for a corner three. *Swish!* We're down one with thirty-five seconds left.

The Rainier Beach coach jumps to his feet to call time, their last. The band is blasting "Shout!" and the people are doing just that, shouting the lyrics as they clap in rhythm. We huddle around Varner. "No need to foul!" he screams. "Tough defense. After we stop them, we'll have at least five seconds. No panic."

The horn sounds, and the band stops.

After Rainier Beach inbounds, we pick their guards up at half-court. The shot clock ticks down. Twenty seconds . . . fifteen . . . ten. With five seconds left on the shot clock and ten seconds left in the game, the ball goes into the corner. Charles jumps out on the Rainier Beach player, and Chambers leaves his man to double-team.

The guy tries a crosscourt pass that Chambers deflects. The ball rolls loose; Charles dives for it and gets it. From the ground he shoves the ball toward Jacobson, who gathers it up and hits me at half-court. I drive toward the hoop, DeSean with me, stride for stride. At the top of the key, I feel Colin trailing the play. I don't know how I know he's there, but I know.

As I go up, DeSean goes up, ready to shove my shot right down my throat and win the game for Rainier Beach. Instead of shooting, I pass to Colin. I'm calling it a pass, but it really isn't. I just sort of drop the ball behind me, knowing Colin will be there. I don't see his shot, because I'm up against the mat behind the hoop when he takes it, but I hear thousands of Rainier Beach fans groan, and then I hear the horn.

Seconds later, guys are jumping all over Colin and then they're jumping all over me and then we're all bouncing around the court, our legs like pogo sticks. Even Flynn Westwood is going nuts. On the bench, Varner has his head down and is sobbing into a towel, Smiley's arm around him.

The Rainier Beach fans are filing out, but our fans have filled the court and are high-fiving one another and letting out rock-concert howls. Somebody grabs me, and I turn around. It's Trey, his eyes as bright as diamonds. "All right, Lucas or Nate, or whoever you are! All right! All right! All right!" He gives me a high five that turns into a hug, and then he disappears into the crowd.

Amelia has a late flight to Oakland, so after the game we drive to the Copperleaf restaurant, this fancy place by Sea-Tac that has great apple pie and ice cream. While we're eating, my mom says she's going to call Grandfather Frick. We all tell her not to. "No," she says. "He's going to eat crow."

After she hangs up, the three of them take turns telling me how great the game was and how great I was. Once the celebration is over, my parents take Amelia to the airport, and we drive home, too tired to talk.

x x x

Hey Lucas—

We won! The game ended a couple of hours ago, but I'm still so sky-high that I feel as if I could float right through the ceiling, sail past the moon, and keep floating until I reach the stars.

I'm so pumped that I'm still wearing my game shoes with your name written on the insoles. I might even sleep with them on. A little weird, I know, but I want this moment to last and last and last.

We did it, bro. We did it.

Nate

36

MONDAY AT SCHOOL, I'M SURROUNDED by kids as soon as I step through the main door. I bump knuckles and get high fives, "Great game!" . . . "Awesome!" . . . "Unbelievable!" At lunch I sit with the team, and we spend the time reliving this play and that play, always coming back to the final play.

There's an assembly at the end of the day, and the gym is packed with students, parents, and ex-players. Ms. Clyburn gives a speech about Coach Varner and his decades of service to the community. When she's finished, she introduces the head of the Metro League, who presents the trophy to Varner. He holds it up over his head, and everybody stands and cheers. Kids start stomping on the bleachers, and Varner has to assume his coach voice to get them to stop.

Once it's quiet, Varner—again fighting back tears—gives a short speech saying that he was blessed to be able to work with such great kids and teachers for so many years. Then he calls the team up to the stage. After we line up, he hands the trophy to Charles, who holds it over his head for a few seconds before he hands it to Colin. One by one, we hold it above our heads as waves of applause roll down from the stands. After that, we get our individual trophies.

The dismissal bell is about to ring, and I can see kids ducking out early as Varner takes the microphone to pass out the remaining trophies. Charles and Colin are co-MVPs; Manny is Most Inspirational. "Last, but not least," Varner says, "our Most Improved Player is Nate Dravus."

When I show the trophies to my parents, they put them both in the center of the mantelpiece above the fireplace. Nobody says anything, but we're all remembering Lucas's MVP trophy in that same spot. They spend dinner talking again about how it was the most exciting game they'd ever seen and how great I'd played.

I nod and smile, but you can't stay in the clouds forever. I do my homework, play some video games, check the NBA scores, shower, and get into bed. I look up at the ceiling. The shadows are there, same as always, but they're just shadows.

x x x

Hey bro—

I know, I know, I know. I haven't written for weeks. I keep meaning to, but I just don't. Even now, I feel like shoving this notebook into my bottom drawer and never looking at it again, but I won't do that.

For the first week after the game, kids would come up to me, bump fists, tell me how exciting everything was, and for a few moments I'd be right with them, reliving the game. In the cafeteria, the guys on the team ate at one table and talked about the title game and the early games and the whole season. I wasn't the emcee or anything, but I joined in.

The second week, I got some smiles and high fives in the hallways, but fewer each day. The talk in the cafeteria moved to other things. Colin got a scholarship offer from Montana and feelers from Oregon State and UNLV, and Charles had schools after him, too. Nevin, Colligan, and Chambers were turning out for baseball, Manny and Jacobson for track. It seemed as if everybody but me was heading in a new direction. I sat through that for a couple of days, wanting to join in, but not able to. When I went back to eating alone, nobody noticed.

I've had two lives—before Nooksack and after Nooksack. That's never going to change. I'm glad I played this season, glad I hung in there for both of us, glad I brought you along on the ride.

But watching shadow games on the ceiling? Telling Trey my name is Lucas? Inventing Carlotta? Sitting alone with my eyes down and my mouth shut? Existing in a permanent fog? I don't want a life of that.

What I want is to go to a community college, maybe study to become a paramedic like the people who tried to save you. I want to go out for the basketball team—just walk on and see what happens. I want to get my driver's license. I want to have real friends and a real girlfriend—normal, everyday stuff.

After you died, I was like a glass that had been dropped from the Space Needle and had shattered into a million pieces. This year, playing basketball, I've glued a few pieces back together, but the glue isn't going to hold. So—that Dr. Gipson I swore that I'd never see? I'm going to go see him.

This time when I talk to him, I'm going to tell him the truth about you and me and Nooksack and everything. I'm thinking that if I don't hold things back, he can get me going forward. The ache inside me is not ever going away, but this is going to be my last letter. I won't forget you, Lucas Cawley, but I've got to get on with it.

My life.

Nate